FATHERSONFATHER

Evan Jacobs

SADDLEBACK
EDUCATIONAL PUBLISHING

Gravel Road

SADDLEBACK
EDUCATIONAL PUBLISHING
www.sdlback.com

Copyright ©2015 by Saddleback Educational Publishing

ISBN-13: 978-1-68021-038-5
ISBN-10: 1-68021-038-6
eBook: 978-1-63078-334-1

Printed in Guangzhou, China
NOR/0715/CA21501108

19 18 17 16 15   1 2 3 4 5

To Mom: How you left this world was much quicker than I could have ever imagined. However, I don't know if all the time in the world would have been enough, or given me what I needed to prepare for it. I think about you constantly.

To Dad: In the beginning we were father and son. By the end, we were as close as two people could be, and I hope you know how much you mean to me. Never forgotten. Ever.

To Andrew: In some ways you're like a brother, in other ways you're like a son, but you're always uniquely you.

This book is also for Shawn. To paraphrase Proverbs, you truly are the "friend that sticketh closer than a brother."

Chapter 1

STAT

Jeff Corman heard the flat voice over the loudspeaker say, "Room 14-B, stat."

Jeff was looking for an information desk. Doctors and nurses were walking around. They were talking to each other. None of them seemed terribly busy for two thirty on a Thursday morning.

"Excuse me," he asked a woman behind the information desk when he finally found it. "Can you tell me where William Corman is?"

The woman looked at him. Her face was blank.

"I'm his son."

Jeff began to reach into his pocket. He was going to show her his driver's license.

"He's in room 14-B." The woman took out a name badge for him. She filled it out.

"Didn't they just call that room number over the loud-speaker?" Jeff was confused.

"Yeah."

"They said room 14-B, stat. What does *stat* mean?"

"Emergency." The woman handed Jeff the name badge.

Jeff sighed and took the badge. He put it on and headed to his father's room. The woman at the desk might have told him which direction to go. But he didn't hear her.

This is bad way to begin my junior year, he thought.

Tomorrow was the second day of the school year. And what a year it was going to be. He had seven classes. He wanted to run for student government as the junior class representative. And he was president of the Key Club. Its members helped people in the community.

Jeff was going to make the most of this school year. He would show whatever colleges he applied to that he was their man.

NOT SUPPOSED TO BE LIKE THIS

Jeff's dad, William, had been sleeping a lot lately. He had a routine. He would get up, shower, dress, and then take a nap. After that he would run a few simple errands, watch TV, and then nap again in the afternoon. Then he would make dinner, or they would go out to eat. He went to bed around nine.

Each night Jeff could hear his dad getting up to use the downstairs bathroom in their small two-story house. Jeff and his dad both used to occupy the upstairs bedrooms. Last year his dad had moved downstairs. Walking up and down the stairs had become too difficult for him.

His dad had Parkinson's disease and his shaking was also worse. His movement had slowed as well. Having diabetes plus a heart condition from thirty years of smoking didn't help. The last five years had all been downhill.

His dad had "gone away" a week before school started. Not physically, but mentally.

They had been sitting in the living room. They were talking about Jeff's schedule for the upcoming semester. Out of nowhere, Mr. Corman stopped talking. He just stared at Jeff, not responding.

"AP Chemistry is gonna suck," Jeff had repeated.

Nothing.

His dad continued to stare at him. Then he began to nod off.

Jeff thought his blood pressure might be low. He gave his dad some food.

That did the trick.

His dad took a nap shortly thereafter and seemed fine. But Jeff wanted him to see his doctor.

"What is he gonna do for me?" Mr. Corman had asked.

Everything was fine for the rest of the week.

Chapter 3

NEW NOT NORMAL

Just two hours before going to the hospital, Jeff was awake, working on an honors English assignment.

He had always been a night owl. He always felt he was different. He figured it probably had something to do with his parents having him as older adults. His dad was forty-nine and his mom was thirty-nine when he was born. People always thought his parents were his grandparents.

He thought he was average looking: tall, dark brown hair, hazel eyes. He seemed to wear the same clothes as everybody else. Jeff didn't think he stood out in any way. He hoped to change that as president of the Key Club. He wanted to be a leader in the community.

When Jeff got to high school, in addition to an always-busy course load, he had to take care of his father more. This didn't help his night owl tendencies. Jeff found it was easier to get work done when his dad was resting or asleep.

That night, Jeff had just gotten ready to go to bed.

Then there was a knock on the front door.

Jeff's dad had mentioned he'd seen blood several times when he used the toilet. He didn't talk much about his health. His dad would sometimes mention an ailment. He would tell Jeff if he felt dizzy. But Jeff wasn't in the loop as far as his dad's medications. His dad didn't talk to him about his numerous doctor's appointments.

Jeff went downstairs.

"Were you the one who called 9-1-1, sir?" Jeff heard an unfamiliar voice ask.

"Dad?" Jeff couldn't believe what he was hearing. His first thought was that maybe somebody had tried to break into their house.

"It's okay," his dad said as he led two muscular men into the living room. Jeff stared at their uniforms. He saw the equipment they held and realized they were paramedics.

They started to check Jeff's father out. They checked his pulse. Then his blood pressure. They asked him some questions.

Jeff's dad was calm. He almost seemed relieved.

It finally dawned on Jeff that his father must have felt awful. The earlier loss of blood and fading out of conversations had scared him enough to call 9-1-1 for help.

Jeff wondered why his father hadn't called him.

Before he could think more about it, a stretcher was wheeled into the house.

"We're gonna lift you up, okay, sir?" one of the EMTs said. "We can't have you climb on. It's a safety issue."

They lifted Jeff's dad onto the stretcher. He was wearing an oxygen mask now.

They started wheeling him out of the house. Jeff felt like they were taking him away forever. He walked with them. He knew where the hospital was. They'd gone there when his mom was sick, before she passed away.

"I'll meet you there, Dad." They looked at each other.

"Okay," his father said.

Jeff noticed the ambulance. There was also a fire truck. *So many first responders*, he thought.

A few neighbors were watching the scene from their windows. A younger couple stood outside.

In moments, Jeff's dad was inside the ambulance. The doors closed and it drove off.

"So I just go to the hospital?" he asked one of the firefighters, who was standing on the front lawn.

"Yeah," he said.

Jeff quickly walked back inside. He was alone. He heard the fire truck start up.

As Jeff got his wallet and keys, he thought, *This isn't happening. This isn't happening. Dad handles all his own medical stuff. He's done it since Mom died. I help around the house and run errands, but that's about it. What if he's really going downhill? What then?*

Jeff started up his car and headed to the emergency room. He felt sick. And he couldn't shake the feeling that he would be seeing a lot more of the hospital.

Chapter 4

ICU

Jeff sat in room 14-B. He thought he might feel stronger if all this was happening in the middle of the school year. Somehow, he felt being halfway through would make things easier to handle.

It was an hour later. His dad had just asked about being released.

"You're blood levels are serious," a nurse said.

The nurse looked at Jeff.

"I can bring your things tomorrow, Dad. You want me to bring your iPad?"

"No." His dad stared vacantly at Jeff.

After talking for a little longer, the nurse left them alone.

"Why didn't you ask me for help? I could've driven you here." Jeff hoped he didn't sound mad.

"I didn't want to bother you." His dad looked at him, then he looked away again.

They chatted for a little bit. Jeff didn't really know what to say. He was trying to be positive.

"They said they're going to give you some blood transfusions." Jeff squeezed his dad's hand. "That will make you feel a lot better. You're blood levels are bad. It's probably why you haven't felt well lately."

Jeff didn't want to remind him about how he'd "gone away."

He could see his dad was tired.

"Why don't you rest? I'll come by before zero period in a few hours."

"Okay." His father yawned.

Jeff hugged him.

"I love you, Dad."

"I love you too."

When Jeff was far down the hall, he looked at his watch. It was just after four in the morning. If he were lucky, he would get a little sleep before he had to go to school.

Chapter 5

DEEPER ENERGY

Jeff woke up at six. He took a quick shower, brushed his teeth, and got dressed. In the kitchen he grabbed two pieces of bread. He wasn't even hungry. But he might be later.

He also got his dad's pillbox. It had a week's worth of medication in it. There were seven small compartments. Each represented one day of the week. And each was filled with pills. Too many pills.

Jeff's dad was sleeping when he got to the ICU. The hospital was very calm as the first rays of light filtered in.

He stared at his dad. He hated seeing him like this. He had been Jeff's hero for many years. His dad had never been an aggressive person. But he was a big man. Now he looked like a balloon slowly leaking air.

A nurse walked into the room. It wasn't the one from a few hours before.

"How is he?" Only then did Jeff notice the machine monitoring his dad's vital signs. He had no idea what the numbers meant. He felt like an idiot. Here he was great at math, science, and English, but he didn't understand a blood-pressure reading. What the numbers actually meant.

"He's still losing blood in his stool. We're going to give him another transfusion later." The nurse was nice. But that didn't make talking to a stranger about his dad any easier.

The nurse left the room.

Jeff didn't understand what was happening. Why was his dad still losing blood? Why couldn't the doctors stop it? Wasn't a hospital where people were supposed to get better?

Jeff stared at his sleeping father a little longer, then he went to school.

Chapter 6

SAFE PLACE

Jeff watched some of the popular kids on campus as he made his way into Miller High School. He knew these kids, but he wasn't really friends with them.

Jeff wasn't tight with anybody. But he had two friends, Brian Kim and Daryl Perez. He mostly hung out with them. He was the closest to Brian, but that wasn't saying much. They had a school friendship.

The three boys did homework together over the phone sometimes. They would go dateless to some school dances. But mostly he saw the guys outside of school only if it was school related: a fundraiser, dance, football game. Even school events were rare for Jeff. Aside from fundraisers and charity drives, Jeff didn't really do anything with anyone but his dad.

Nobody knew about his dad's condition. It wasn't

because Jeff didn't want to tell people. He didn't think they would care. Everybody was so busy. There was schoolwork and college entrance exams. Way more important stuff to talk and think about than Parkinson's.

Even Jeff had put off thinking about how sick his father was becoming. His dad had been getting around okay. Jeff knew it was going to be different now. He didn't know how different, but he just knew it was not going to be the same.

Jeff saw two people kissing as he turned a corner toward his calculus classroom.

He'd never had a real girlfriend either. He'd dated a little bit, but it was never anything serious.

Jeff's mom died at the end of his sixth-grade year. She'd had a rare heart condition. The doctor's didn't diagnose it until it was too late. She went into the hospital with chest pains and never came out.

Despite everything, Jeff was happy to be at school. He knew what to expect.

Chapter 7

IN A SECOND

Jeff went to the hospital during lunch. Despite not getting any sleep, he felt okay.

He passed some other rooms in the ICU. He couldn't help but peek as he walked by. Family members were gathered together. They stood around the beds of people who seemed very ill, maybe dying.

Jeff looked away. He didn't want anybody staring at him and his dad.

"Normally a colonoscopy is a very routine procedure. Doing one will help us better understand your blood loss," Dr. Patel was saying as Jeff walked in. "But, Mr. Corman, you have done a great deal of damage to your body. Your years of smoking, coupled with your blood loss ..."

The doctor pointed to an intravenous fluid pump. His father's blood transfusion.

"This is your fifth transfusion," he said. The doctor sounded like he was scolding his dad. Jeff felt himself getting tight inside. He didn't like hearing his father be treated like a little kid. "Your body is still experiencing a loss. That makes putting you under for a colonoscopy a bigger risk."

Jeff looked at his dad. He was doing the thing where he looked like he was listening, but he wasn't. He seemed to be thinking about something.

He guessed it was about dying. Death.

He realized they were having *that* talk now. He wasn't in any way prepared for it. He knew his dad wasn't well, but was he about to die?

The doctor left the room. Jeff and his father looked at each other.

"Well, Jeff, I took you as far as I could."

"Dad." Jeff didn't want to come down on his father. But he couldn't help being angry.

"You heard the doctor." His dad stared at Jeff. Then he looked away.

"Yeah, but he didn't tell you not to do the procedure. You need to do it so they can find out what's wrong with you."

Jeff's dad nodded his head. He still didn't look at him.

Jeff watched his father for what felt like forever.

"So, you're gonna do it?" Jeff finally asked.

His dad nodded his head. But he still didn't look at his son.

Jeff didn't understand where his own presence of mind was coming from. How he was able to think at all. He just knew he had to. Because if he didn't, he wouldn't have a parent left.

One of them had to make the important decisions.

Chapter 8

UP AND BACK

Jeff got back to school late. His English teacher, Mrs. Reisbaum, didn't seem to notice.

She was talking about the book *The Catcher in the Rye*. It was the first book the junior honors class was going to read that semester. Jeff had read it over the summer.

He'd loved it. He loved how free the main character, Holden Caulfield, was. He loved how he could do whatever he wanted.

Jeff took notes in class, like it was any other day. He even contributed to the discussion.

But he couldn't stop thinking about his dad.

"Calc tonight," a text from Brian said. They were going to do homework via video chat.

"Sure," Jeff replied.

After school he returned to the hospital. His father was still in the ICU.

Jeff heard talking as he approached his dad's room. He walked in and saw Debra and Duane Goldberg. They were family friends. Jeff had slept at their house many times when he was younger. He'd played with their kids. They were about the same age.

Then Jeff's mom died. And the Goldbergs—like a lot of family friends—disappeared. Jeff's dad hadn't kept up with them. He wasn't a great communicator, and they didn't seem to understand that about him.

"You're mother and I would do things with them as a couple," his dad would say if Jeff pushed him to call. "You don't understand."

Jeff knew his dad was partly to blame. Still, he couldn't help being angry at them. He felt like they had abandoned his dad.

His father's best friend, Cliff Perkins, had told the Goldbergs about his condition. Cliff wasn't the warmest person, but he was always there for Jeff's dad. He was in the hospital room too.

The Goldbergs were happy to see Jeff. They asked all the usual questions people ask a junior in high school.

"How is school?"

"What college do you want to go to?"

Then they told Jeff about their kids, Jeff's old friends. It felt like years since he'd spoken to any of them.

Jeff listened and nodded his head. But he didn't hear any of it. He didn't care.

All he wanted was for his dad to be okay.

When they left, Jeff felt bitter. Like they had put in their time. They didn't even ask who was taking care of him.

"See you tomorrow," Jeff's dad told Cliff, who left a few minutes later.

"I wouldn't miss it," Cliff said. He shook Jeff's hand. "You got a good kid here, William."

"I know." Jeff's dad stared at him.

He didn't smile. He didn't do anything. Jeff figured he was too nervous.

Chapter 9

JUST THE TWO OF US

Well, you know where the money is if something happens." Jeff's dad stared at him.

Jeff sat across from the bed. The only other sound in the room was coming from the machines monitoring vital signs.

For the first time, Jeff noticed the bedpans and urine containers. Could his dad still get up to use the bathroom by himself? Jeff figured they were there in case he couldn't get help in time.

"Yeah." He knew his dad was talking about his retirement accounts. He didn't know what he would do with the money. He didn't know how much money was there. He wasn't even sure how to get it.

"Cliff will help you," his dad said, as if he were reading his mind. "I love you, Jeff."

"I love you too, Dad."

Jeff's dad squeezed his hand. Jeff took a deep breath. He felt himself starting to lose it. His body tensed up to stop the coming tears. He didn't want to cry in front of his dad.

"Everything's going to be okay, Dad."

"I'm still losing blood. Even after five pints, I'm still losing it."

Jeff didn't have any answers. He felt bad. All he could do was sit with his dad. Keep him company.

He was almost seventeen. This made Jeff even angrier about the situation. How could he be expected to have everything figured out? Nobody had asked him how he was handling it.

Chapter 10

LONG WALK TO THE PARKING LOT

Jeff put on a brave face. The bravest he had ever had to wear. He told his dad to rest. He told him he would be by in the morning before school. The colonoscopy was scheduled shortly after Jeff's zero period class. He gave his dad a hug and left the room.

Jeff walked past all the other rooms in the ICU. He didn't look at anyone as he left the hospital. He continued walking toward the parking lot, keeping his head down. It was dark outside. Every so often a passing car's headlights highlighted his feet.

Then Jeff got in his car and started bawling. None of this was unexpected. That was what really bothered him.

He knew his dad, with Parkinson's disease, diabetes, and all those years of smoking, wasn't going to live forever.

Jeff had hoped his father could make it through his senior year of high school. Maybe even see him graduate from college and get married. Then if his condition got worse, he would at least know Jeff had made a life for himself. His own life.

But it was not looking good. His dad was only sixty-five.

He's not that old! Jeff wanted to scream.

But he didn't. What good would that do him?

Chapter 11

DANIELLE

In all the drama about the colonoscopy, Jeff realized he never returned to school. He told himself to not worry about it. Jeff had never been flakey with his schoolwork or club commitments. Mr. McDonald, the Key Club advisor, liked Jeff. He wouldn't give him a hard time for missing a club meeting.

Then he realized he hadn't contacted his uncles—his father's brothers—Lenny and Nicholas. Jeff called them when he got home. He got their voice mail both times and left messages.

Jeff had his iPad next to his calculus homework. He was video chatting with Brian.

"Danielle wants you to take her to the homecoming dance," Brian said.

Jeff almost choked on the ramen noodles he'd made.

"No way." Jeff laughed.

Jeff saw Brian's mom walk by in the background. That upset him for a second.

His dad wasn't there. His dad might never come home again. The house was empty.

"Why?" Brian broke into his thoughts. "She's hot, and she'd probably bone you, dude."

"Yeah, who hasn't she boned?" Jeff didn't need to worry about his volume. Brian was using his earbuds. "You even hooked up with her."

"That was for like half a minute, dude." Brian cracked up.

It may have seemed like half a minute to Brian, but Jeff remembered it. Since middle school Danielle Herrera had dated almost everybody Jeff knew. But she'd never shown the faintest interest in him.

Jeff acted like he didn't care. But he did. He'd always thought Danielle was beautiful. She had long, thick dirty blonde hair. Her skin was tan, and it got even darker in the summer. She had striking brown eyes with incredibly long lashes. Jeff always wanted those eyes to look at him in that special way. But they never had.

Jeff put her out of his mind. He had school, his clubs, and his dad.

That was enough for Jeff Corman to think about. Even though he had to see her every day, Jeff's daily life made her easy to forget.

How could he take Danielle seriously now? Why did she want to be with him? So she could check off his name from her list?

"No, thanks," Jeff said.

Chapter 12

UNCLE LENNY

Jeff and Brian were done with their calculus homework earlier than expected. Normally, Jeff would have seen if his dad needed anything after finishing his assignments. But then again, he would have started his schoolwork later too. Tonight, he had freedom. He could work with Brian whenever he wanted.

And Jeff loved it.

He also hated that he loved it. He hated how good it felt not to run errands and watch out for his dad.

Before he could think too long, Uncle Lenny returned his call.

"A colonoscopy?" Uncle Lenny seemed almost speechless after being debriefed about Jeff's dad. "That's a regular procedure. It's not surgery. It shouldn't be a big deal, Jeff."

"He's been losing so much blood. They're worried about how he's going to respond to the anesthesia," Jeff said.

His uncles didn't live nearby. They didn't see Jeff's dad often. They weren't very involved. Jeff realized nobody—other than him—had any idea just how sick William Corman was.

Chapter 13

MORNING OF

I've told your dad and I'm telling you," Cliff said as soon as Jeff entered the hospital room. Jeff had no idea how long Cliff had been there. "I don't think he should go through with the procedure. He's too weak."

"We have to do something," Jeff said.

He felt the warming rays of the sun through the window as it began to rise. Jeff would've given anything to be out watching it. To be a little kid again. Not having to deal with anything medical. Like how it was when his mom was alive.

Jeff looked at his dad. He looked the same. He was lying on the hospital bed. Presumably thinking about everything. Next to him were some empty bottles. Jeff figured they were what the nursing staff made you drink before a colonoscopy.

The machines continued to make their routine noises. They continued to monitor his dad.

"And you shouldn't go to school today. This is a family crisis. The school will understand," Cliff went on.

Jeff didn't know how to respond. Cliff was always lecturing. Always giving advice. His dad seemed to listen until Cliff changed the subject.

Then Jeff had a thought. He wanted say, *If you care so much, Cliff, then you should be more involved. You should take Dad to the doctor. You should push him to do more. And stop telling me what to do all the time.*

But Jeff knew Cliff did what he could. He did have to live his own life.

"I don't want him to stay here," Jeff's dad finally said. "Jeff needs to go to school. I'll be fine."

"Well, I'll call you immediately after the procedure to let you know how it went." Cliff held up his phone.

Jeff wanted to talk more to his dad. Say something profound. Instead, he shook Cliff's hand. Then he gave his dad a hug and left.

When Jeff got to his car he sat down, put on the seat belt, and started crying again. Sobs wracked his body. It was hard. It was concentrated. He felt like he couldn't breathe.

Jeff continued to cry.

Then he eyed the clock. Eighteen minutes before school started. He turned on the car.

This was all he could do. It was all he had left.

Chapter 14

ALWAYS THE WRONG TIME

Hey, stranger." Danielle smiled as she nudged Jeff. He moved slightly so she wouldn't get too close. She wore a black tank top and jeans. It was still summer weather. Despite not wanting to be touched, he thought she looked great.

Jeff had checked his phone all morning. No call from Cliff.

He was not focused on Danielle. His thoughts were with his father. Plus he had an upcoming meeting with Mr. McDonald. Jeff wanted to go over the fundraisers the students had planned for the fall semester.

"Hey." Jeff looked at Danielle.

She had a devilish smile on her face. She always seemed to wear it.

He could hardly look at her. Now that she was interested in him. Now that he was the last of her choices.

"How do you like being a junior?" she asked.

"School just started." Jeff really hoped she'd walk away. That she'd find somebody else to talk to.

"Are you going to the homecoming dance?"

"Nope," he said.

"Would you go if you had a date?" Danielle was weaving her web. Jeff wasn't going to be caught in it.

"I don't have a date," he said.

Jeff could feel Danielle eyeing him. It was like she was staring through him.

"Well …" Danielle took a deep breath. "Since you can't take a hint, I want to go to the dance with you."

"Why?" He looked at her. Her devilish smile had faded.

"You need to relax more." Danielle didn't look away. She knew the power of her gaze. "It's our junior year. Nobody ever sees you except at school. You need to stop being so busy and have fun."

Hearing that made Jeff angry.

People knew his dad wasn't well. None of them knew how sick he really was. None of them knew that "fun" wasn't on Jeff's radar right now. It didn't matter how much people told him it should be.

"I'll talk to you later," he said.

Jeff walked up to Mr. McDonald's classroom. He quickly went inside, pulling the door firmly shut behind him.

Chapter 15

THE CALL

So, everything went fine," Dr. Patel said. Cliff had called when the doctor was in the room. He had put the doctor on the phone. "But your father has severe diverticulitis. He should avoid popcorn, seeds, and small things that can lodge themselves in the pockets of the colon."

"Is he still losing blood?" Jeff asked. The fourth period bell was going to ring in a few minutes.

"Not at this time."

"What about his heart? Is there anything we can do to make it work better?" Jeff felt like an idiot. He was only a teen. He didn't know the right way to ask about his father's condition.

"Well, as you know, your father has angina. According to his medical records, he had a stent put in about twenty years ago. I would recommend another one to increase blood flow. But your father's arteries are too blocked. I don't think it would do him much good. In fact, it might do more harm."

"Oh." Jeff didn't really understand what Dr. Patel said. He just knew his dad's heart wasn't going to get any better.

"We are going to keep him overnight. He should be able to go home tomorrow. Okay?"

"Okay," Jeff said.

He was nervous. What if his dad wasn't ready to come home?

Chapter 16

RAISED STAKES

As the day went on, Jeff realized he wasn't nervous about his father's health. Now that he was stable. But he was bummed because his dad was coming home.

Jeff Corman's brief moment of freedom was gone. The past day, as nerve-racking as it had been, was the most free time he'd had in a long while.

He felt awful for feeling this way. He hated that he liked being alone. He told himself to stop thinking about it. He had to focus on his father.

When Jeff got the hospital, Cliff was there. The curtain in the room was pulled around the bed.

"He's going to the bathroom." Cliff laughed.

"Oh." Jeff stared at the curtain. He wanted to know why his dad wasn't in a real bathroom. Then he figured it was probably because he was too weak to walk there.

"He hasn't started bleeding again," Cliff said. "In total, they had to give him seven pints of blood."

Jeff heard his dad laugh.

"Hey, Dad," Jeff said.

"I know, I know, you keep saying that. I'm just glad I'm not bleeding anymore," Jeff's dad replied.

Jeff got nervous. His dad was talking to him in a way that didn't make sense. Had he "gone away" again? So soon?

"He's on the phone with your uncle Nicholas," Cliff said.

Jeff shook his head.

He honestly couldn't believe what was happening. His dad was always on him about spraying after he used the bathroom. He lectured him about not staying in there too long. Now his dad was essentially going to the bathroom in front of Jeff and Cliff. And he was talking on his cell phone!

Jeff was embarrassed. He wanted this situation to be over.

"Your dad is one lucky customer," Cliff said. "He thought he was gonna die. I did too."

"Yeah." Jeff couldn't understand how easily Cliff could say these things.

"You need to get that stubborn SOB to exercise more. You also need to help him stay on top of his meds and doctor's appointments. Your dad can't do it all."

Jeff nodded his head. He wanted to ask Cliff for more help. He wanted to tell him that he couldn't live his life *and* his dad's life too.

Nobody seemed to want to hear that.

Jeff's dad laughed at something Uncle Nicholas said on the other end of the phone. Then he hung up. "Okay," his father said. "I'm done."

"Any more blood?" Cliff asked.

"None."

Jeff could hear the smile in his dad's voice. Cliff smiled. Jeff smiled too, despite feeling completely miserable and grossed out.

Chapter 17

FOOD

Get healthy foods," Jeff's dad had said. He didn't know what that meant. Jeff was walking listlessly around the supermarket.

He had grocery shopped with his dad a lot in the past. They always went in the early evening. Right when Jeff got home from school. His dad was tired and didn't move well. So lugging groceries took a lot out of him. Sometimes, when his dad had to shop by himself, he would take a nap before putting the groceries away.

Jeff had so many thoughts in his head as he tried to look for "healthy foods."

Dad is going to need more care. He'll need more of my time. I don't know how I'm going to get everything done. I can barely take care of myself. All that matters is that Dad's okay. I shouldn't be so selfish.

As he looked around the store, he couldn't make up his mind about what was or wasn't healthy. Sure, he had been food shopping a million times, but he just pushed the cart. He didn't really pay attention.

Now his dad was sicker than ever.

Was there anything Jeff could buy that was going to help him get well?

Eventually, he left the store. He basically bought everything he'd seen his father buy before.

Chapter 18

UNCLE NICHOLAS

You seem like you're handling everything okay," Uncle Nicholas said in a slow, measured tone. He was finally returning Jeff's call. Jeff was in the middle of his chemistry homework.

Uncle Nicholas and Uncle Lenny were really smart. Uncle Nicholas was a writer. He wrote for financial magazines. Uncle Lenny was a professor of computer science.

Before he stopped working, Jeff's dad had been a freelance graphic designer.

Jeff had told Uncle Nicholas the whole story. His uncle had questions. Medical questions. Jeff didn't have answers.

"I could give you the number of Dr. Patel," Jeff offered.

"Yeah, could you do that?"

This was exactly what Jeff wanted. Let the adults deal with it. Get the people who knew what they were doing talking. He didn't like the weight of such responsibility.

He was only sixteen. Jeff could fetch things around the house. He could run errands. He didn't know anything about medical procedures and medication. His dad had never told him.

Now Jeff felt like he was up against the clock of his father's health. And he didn't have time to learn.

They talked a bit more. Uncle Nicholas wanted to know about school. Where was Jeff planning on going to college? Was he was dating anyone?

Jeff liked his uncles. He knew they would do whatever they could to help. Jeff needed more help and he knew it. He and his dad had probably needed more help for a while.

Chapter 19

PERSISTENT DANIELLE

You're going with me to the dance next Friday." Danielle bumped softly into Jeff as she said that.

They were walking through the high school campus.

She was wearing a black sundress. Her freshly showered hair smelled great. Her body felt good against his.

Still, Jeff tensed up and moved away. It was easy for him to ignore her. He had only gotten four hours of sleep.

And it wasn't because of his dad. It was because he wanted to get ahead on his schoolwork. He had to. He had to be ready in case something happened to his father again.

It was the only control Jeff felt he had.

"I'm gonna pick you up." Danielle smiled at him. "All you have to do is get dressed. Or not."

She laughed.

Jeff hated it.

He hated that she could laugh. That everybody could laugh and have fun.

Even more, he hated that he couldn't enjoy being a teenager.

I have to stay with my dad. I have to find out about his meds. I have to get in touch with his doctors, he wanted to tell Danielle.

Jeff knew she wouldn't care.

Everybody was happy. Nobody wanted to think about sad things when they were happy.

Danielle had kept on him. She obviously wanted to go to the dance with him. He wanted to tell her to stop wasting her time.

I'm not interested. Just leave me alone, he wanted to scream.

But he was interested. Which made him even angrier. Because he didn't feel like he could do anything about it.

"Okay," Jeff said.

"We're going?" Danielle seemed surprised. "I'll call you later and we'll set everything up." She squeezed his arm as she walked off. "Bye, Jeff."

Danielle was a dream girl for Jeff. He was turned on by everything about her. Her looks, her personality, her voice ... EVERYTHING.

But this was no dream. He was living a nightmare.

Chapter 20

CHANGE OF PLANS

They think it would be better if I went to Building Up to rest," Jeff's dad had said on the phone.

Jeff was driving over to the hospital to pick him up.

"Wait? What? Who thinks that? How long will you be there?" Jeff was confused. He felt like his dad was being taken away from him. "What's Building Up?"

"It's a place where people go to rest. Get better."

"Why not just come home?" A chill went through Jeff's body. He had heard something on the news about people like his father being taken advantage of.

"Just meet me there. They're getting ready to take me over. It's close to the house. Near Brookhurst."

"Okay. I'll look it up. See you soon."

His father hung up the phone.

Chapter 21

BUILDING UP

From the outside Building Up looked like a big apartment complex. There were many windows. In the center of the building was a set of entry doors that opened and closed automatically.

Jeff parked far away from the entrance. As he approached, he saw a group of people standing on the side of the building. They were smoking. They wore baggy shirts, baggy shorts, and sweatpants. Many of them were skinny and frail. They all had liver spots on their hands and arms. One of them was missing his legs.

As Jeff walked through the door, he realized what Building Up really was. A hotel for sick people. Inside was worse.

Older people who could barely stand used walkers or were assisted by nurses. There were doctors and nurses talking in small groups. There were visitors milling about.

Carts of food were being wheeled around. People were lying down in their beds, letting the streams of daytime TV wash over them. Random sick people were sitting in the hallway. Some were nodding off. Others were checked out.

One was even arguing with a nurse that he wanted to go home. "I'm gonna sue this whole place if you don't let me go home," he kept saying.

Jeff found his dad's room: 1012.

He had gotten it from the front desk. Jeff was supposed to get a name badge, but he didn't. No one had even bothered to check his ID.

BAND-AID

Jeff found his dad resting in his double room, eating lunch. He had soup, a turkey sandwich, and a fruit cup. They had also given him a diet Coke.

There was a very old Asian man in the other bed. He was sleeping.

Both TVs in the room were on.

"Medicare covers this for up to three weeks," Jeff's dad said. He seemed to be in a good mood. Comfortable. That made Jeff feel better.

"So, you're okay being here?" Jeff just wanted his dad to be happy. He would feel better about his dad being in a place like Building Up if he was relaxed.

"Oh yeah. I won't be here long. It's probably better if I am feeling weak. If I'm here, then you won't have to take care of me. You shoulda seen the lady they sent to talk to me about coming here." His dad looked at Jeff.

"Why?" Jeff laughed. He was starting to feel better about the situation. His dad was acting like his old self.

"This gorgeous blonde comes in. She starts telling me about this place." His dad had a big smile. He was enjoying telling his son this story. "She told me Medicare would cover a visit to a place like this. She said my doctor thought I should go."

Jeff felt a hand on his shoulder. He looked up. The Asian man had gotten out of bed. He was talking to Jeff in a foreign language.

"What does he want?" Jeff's dad inquired.

"I don't know. I can't understand him." Jeff felt bad saying that. He felt bad that he couldn't help him.

Eventually, the Asian man wandered out the door.

Jeff started to leave an hour later. As he did, a woman walked into the room. She moved quickly and with purpose.

The more he looked at her, the more he noticed she was different. She was tall and muscular. She had strong hands and a strong chin. Her face didn't seem to match her long red hair. She wore blue scrubs. Her name badge read Andrea.

"Are you Mr. Corman's son?" Andrea's voice sounded like a woman's. It was singsong. However, it was deep. Too deep.

"Yeah," Jeff said uncomfortably.

Andrea shook Jeff's hand. She had a strong grip. Stronger than any girl's.

"I'm Andrea. I'm going to be your dad's nurse. Don't worry. We're gonna take great care him."

Andrea smiled at Jeff and walked over to his dad. Jeff could tell Andrea knew he knew something was different about her. At the same time, Andrea didn't seem to care.

That bothered him.

"Mr. Corman, can I get you anything?"

"No, I'm fine."

"Bye, Dad," Jeff said as he was halfway out the door.

"Bye."

Jeff moved down the corridor of Building Up again. He could still hear Andrea talking to his father. He was happy his dad was here. He was happy his father was going to be okay. At least for the moment.

But he couldn't stop thinking about Andrea. He couldn't stop thinking about what he thought "she" was.

Chapter 23

PHO

Danielle's gonna molest you!" Daryl Perez laughed.

Jeff, Brian, and Daryl had gone to lunch at Pho You. It was a Vietnamese noodle restaurant. Jeff always got the same thing, noodles with shrimp.

"I doubt it," Jeff said. He had been so busy he hadn't canceled the homecoming dance with Danielle yet. It was Monday. The dance was Friday. Jeff told himself to cancel tonight. After visiting his dad at Building Up.

Part of him just wanted to go. If all Danielle wanted was a hookup, why couldn't he do that? Why couldn't he just be with her?

Because he wanted more than that. Because his life was already complicated enough. The last thing he needed was Danielle having something on him.

What if they actually started going out? How would Jeff fit that in?

Tony Munigi walked in. He was with his boyfriend, Denny Parker. They had never come out as a couple, but everybody knew they were.

Brian and Daryl looked at each other. Then they looked at Jeff and tried not to crack up.

"There's your friend, Jeff." Brian smiled at him.

"I haven't talked to him since fifth grade," Jeff said.

"Why?" Daryl's eyes narrowed. "Something happen between you two?"

"He told me he liked *you* more than me." Jeff smiled.

"Burn! Jeff wins." Brian laughed.

They continued to eat and watch Tony and Denny.

"You know what's crazy?" Daryl took a sip of his soda. "Even in fifth grade we knew about Tony. Just the way he was. Like we knew he wasn't a real boy."

MR. SONG

Jeff didn't see his dad. He was always in his bed whenever Jeff came to visit. His heart started to race.

He moved into the room. He saw the impression in the bed left by his dad's body.

Then he saw Mr. Song. He was on the floor. He was sitting up against the bed. He looked up at Jeff and smiled.

"Hi, Mr. Song," Jeff said.

They had never been introduced. Jeff just heard the nurses calling him that.

Mr. Song glanced at Jeff. Then he spoke in the language Jeff didn't understand. He held out his arms. Jeff reached for them.

"Did you fall down again, Mr. Song?" a nurse asked. Jeff looked over at her. She had her hands on her hips. She was acting like she was more upset than she was. "I tell you, I don't know what I'm gonna do with you," she said, wagging her finger.

She moved in front of Jeff and helped Mr. Song up. She put him back in bed.

"Excuse me," Jeff finally said. The nurse looked at him like this was the first time she had noticed he was there. "Do you know where William Corman is? He's in the other bed."

"Oh, the lovely Mr. Corman," the nurse said as she helped Mr. Song get comfortable. "Andrea took him to PT."

PT? Jeff didn't know what that meant.

"Physical therapy." The nurse smiled, as if she were reading his mind.

"Okay, thank you." Jeff headed for the door.

He figured he would leave. Jeff had tried to see his dad, but he wasn't available. He would come back later tonight. He started to think about what he was going to do with his free time.

"You should go watch him," the nurse said.

Jeff turned and looked at her.

"You can cheer him on. Just make a right and keep walking. It's at the end of the hall."

MAN-CHILD

Jeff didn't walk into the physical therapy room. He watched his dad "work out" with Andrea through a small window in the door.

His dad was walking slowly between two poles. Andrea walked behind him. She held a large belt around his waist.

Jeff was fixated on Andrea's arms. The way they flexed. Their muscle tone. He'd never seen a woman who was built like that.

At that moment he knew he was right. Andrea wasn't really a woman. At least she hadn't been born that way. She was a guy.

Right then, Andrea looked through the window. She saw Jeff and smiled. She waved him in. That's when Jeff saw his father's face. It was really pale. There was a layer of sweat on it.

Jeff wanted him to rest. He knew Andrea was pushing him too hard. Jeff started breathing harder and faster. "Let him rest!" he declared as he burst into the PT room.

Andrea grabbed a towel from a nearby bench. Jeff's dad was steadying himself on one of the poles. Andrea wiped down his father's face.

"We're done," she said cheerfully.

Everybody in the room seemed to be looking at Jeff.

"You know what they say." Jeff's dad smiled. "No pain, no gain."

Everybody in the room laughed.

Except Jeff.

Chapter 26

NARC

Give Andrea some more time," Mrs. Ward, the social worker for Building Up, said. She was blonde and professionally dressed. The way she spoke made everything sound easy.

"Is she supposed to push my father like that?" Jeff was mad. He didn't want Andrea taking care of his father.

He hated everything about her. Her smug demeanor. Her fake smile. Her—

"This is a rehabilitative facility. Has your father complained about her?"

Jeff shook his head.

"She's very good at what she does. She has an almost one hundred percent success rate in rehabilitating patients. They often times leave here in even better shape than before they got sick. Andrea gets requested more than any other nurse."

The social worker looked at him. Jeff knew she knew they didn't have a lot of money. There was no way they could afford to sue this place to stop Andrea from working with his dad.

"Okay, but if my dad complains about her, I want him being taken care of by somebody else." He felt weird making this demand. He was only sixteen years old, but he was telling an adult what to do.

"That's fine." Mrs. Ward smiled.

Jeff was still angry. He wanted to know why Andrea was working there. Why someone who was like that could be allowed to be around normal people. He knew she had a right to a job. He just didn't like that it was with his dad.

As Jeff was leaving, he saw Andrea and his father. They were walking toward his room.

He thought about saying goodbye to his dad. He wanted to talk to Andrea. To tell her to ease up.

Then he realized it was only five o'clock. He didn't have any homework. He had no commitments. For the moment he was free.

He didn't want to let that freedom go.

Chapter 27

TOO BUSY TO FLAKE

Jeff had been so busy with his dad and school that he never canceled his date with Danielle.

That's how he found himself getting ready for the homecoming dance that Friday evening. With every layer of clothing he put on, with every comb of his hair, Jeff was getting angrier.

Why am I doing this? I need to be doing something to help my dad. This is so ridiculous, he thought.

Their house was a mess. He wasn't a messy person. But it was always this way. His dad never threw anything out. There was mail, newspapers, dust, and clutter all over the place. The house didn't look dirty, but it didn't look clean either.

Just thinking about the mess was making him angry. He wanted to be straightening up. In some way, Jeff felt that cleaning the house would make everything better. If the house were clean, life would be too.

"Looking good, Corman," Danielle said as she forced her way inside. Jeff had tried to avoid it. He wanted to go to her house, but she insisted on picking him up. "Since you don't want to go with me," she had joked. She probably thought he would flake.

Jeff watched her look around the living room. There were old newspapers and mail in a large stack on the floor. The mess was leaning against the large recliner Jeff's dad always sat in. It was right in front of the TV. There was a couch across from it.

Despite not wanting to go to the dance, he couldn't ignore how good Danielle looked. She was wearing a long-sleeve black dress. Her blonde hair looked bright and shiny against it. Jeff wondered how many guys she had worn that dress for. She had really glammed up tonight.

He was wearing an off-white dress shirt and some brown corduroy pants.

"Brian told me about your dad." Danielle looked at him. For a brief moment she had caught Jeff admiring her.

He hadn't told Brian much. Just that his dad had gone to the hospital for a while.

"He's away on business," Jeff said. It was a quick lie. An easy lie. He wouldn't speak to her again after the dance anyway.

"So he's doing better?" Danielle eyed the dusty coffee

table. On it was a blood pressure monitor. Next to it was a list of medications. Jeff made a mental note to look it over.

"My grandpa had one of those." Danielle picked up the blood pressure monitor. She looked at it, as if she were thinking about her grandfather. "When he used to live with us."

"My dad was sick but he's better now," Jeff offered quickly. He didn't want to know too much about Danielle. He didn't want to care. He couldn't afford to care.

Danielle locked eyes with him. It was like once she had him in his gaze, he couldn't look away. Even though he wanted to.

"That's great." She smiled.

Jeff knew she didn't believe him.

Chapter 28

BLOWING IT

Some hip-hop music was playing in Danielle's car. Jeff noticed the car was super clean. It smelled like Danielle, which meant that it smelled like her hair. Despite his mood, it was awesome.

"Sierra's gonna have some people over after." Danielle glanced at Jeff. He was trying not to look at her. "Don't worry, it won't be one of her famous make-out parties."

Danielle laughed. Jeff smiled mildly. She nudged him with her elbow. "Unless you want it to be."

Sierra's make-out parties were the kind of parties Jeff and his friends wanted to be invited to. They were filled with easy hookups. But now it wasn't even worth it.

Danielle continued to talk. Jeff gave one-word answers. She made jokes. Jeff didn't laugh. Eventually, she was the only one talking.

Then he yawned. He was tired. He still wasn't sleeping much.

Danielle pulled her car over.

"Okay," she said. "If you want me to take you home, I'll take you home. I can't make you to have a good time. I know I forced you to hang out tonight. I thought you might lighten up. Maybe we could talk, and I could get to know you more. But, Jeff, I really don't want to spend all night having a bad time trying to make you happy."

"Thank you."

Danielle shook her head. Jeff knew it was a mean thing to say.

"You think I've been with all of your friends, huh?" she asked.

He shook his head. He knew she didn't believe him.

"You know, you don't know anything about me, but you're judging me." Danielle sounded truly hurt. She was not acting like the carefree party girl with the devilish look everybody saw at school. "And all I know about you is that you work really hard in school. And that your dad is sick."

Sick? Jeff wanted to tell her that his father was a lot more than sick.

"How can anybody help you if you don't talk about it?" Danielle stared at him.

Jeff wanted her to look away. But he knew she wouldn't. So he was going to have to hurt her feelings even more.

"I thought you were taking me home." His eyes met hers. He didn't look away.

He hated hurting somebody who was trying to help him.

She turned the car around and drove in complete silence.

After Danielle dropped him off, he thought cleaning would make him feel better. It didn't. For too long his dad had let stuff sit. Things were dusty and gross. Making matters worse, Jeff didn't know what his dad did and didn't need.

So he didn't end up cleaning at all. For a millisecond he thought about texting Danielle. But he didn't do that either. He didn't do anything.

Chapter 29

WEEKEND BLUES

If Jeff thought Building Up was depressing during the week, he found it even worse on the weekend.

The sun was shining. It would've been a great day to go out with his friends. Or even see Danielle. They hadn't talked since the aborted dance date. He hadn't really even seen her at school.

Both TVs in the room were on. Mr. Song's family was there. They were all talking at once. Jeff thought maybe the language was Chinese.

"So, Andrea will be coming by the house twenty-five hours a week. For how long?" Jeff's bad mood was getting even worse.

His dad was going to be coming home next week. A government program was funding Andrea's work hours.

She was going to take him to his medical appointments, cook, help him exercise, and do anything else he needed.

Making Jeff even more uncomfortable was that his dad had requested Andrea as his aide.

"You should be happy. Now we have help." Jeff's dad and Andrea had formed a bond. He really liked her.

Doesn't it bother you that she used to be a man? That she's a man acting like a girl? he wanted to scream.

Jeff's dad didn't care. Andrea was just Andrea.

"Cliff likes her too." His dad smiled. "They're always making jokes."

The more Jeff's dad spoke, the more pissed off he got. *He* could take care of his dad. He'd give up even more of his time. Maybe Cliff would help.

"Hello, Mr. Song!" Andrea glowed as she came into the room.

Jeff watched her as she spoke with Mr. Song's family. Jeff hated the way she carried herself. He hated how obvious it was that Andrea was a man. He hated that nobody but him seemed to notice. That nobody but him seemed to care.

Most of all, he hated Andrea's smile. To Jeff, it was the cherry on top of the lie Andrea was telling everybody. That Andrea was telling herself.

"Looking good, Mr. Corman," Andrea said when she came over.

"I feel pretty good." Jeff's dad smiled.

There was a pause. Jeff looked at the cream-colored floor tile.

"Hi, Jeff," Andrea offered.

"Hey." Jeff wanted her to leave him alone. He thought if he was cold and rude, then maybe she would go away. Maybe she would ask not to work in his house.

"Teenagers." Jeff's dad laughed.

Jeff looked at him. He felt betrayed. It was like his dad was siding with Andrea against him.

"It has nothing to do with being a teenager," Jeff said rudely. He still wasn't looking at Andrea.

"Then what is it?" Andrea's tone was light, but her voice was firm.

Jeff shook his head.

"Jeff, can I talk to you in the hallway?" she asked.

Jeff stared Andrea straight in the eye. If she wanted a fight. If she wanted to know what was on his mind. Then she was going to hear it. He didn't *need* Andrea. He could take care of his dad just fine without her.

"Sure."

Chapter 30

BLAST

You really need to see me as an ally," Andrea said.

Jeff was seething. She was still trying to pull her phony ray-of-sunshine act over on him.

"I know it's been the two of you for a very long time. Ever since your dear mother passed away. I know that can be hard to let go of."

"That's not it." He was going for it. He wanted to let Andrea know he didn't like what she was. Then maybe she wouldn't come to his house.

"What is it, then?" Andrea seemed ready.

Jeff stared at her. He was at a loss for words. He knew why Andrea made him uncomfortable. That didn't mean it was easy to say.

"Is it seeing your father give up control of his life?"

"No." Jeff knew Andrea knew this was part of it. But it wasn't the main reason.

"Oh." Andrea smiled a little, then she composed herself. "It's because I'm a transgender person." She looked into his eyes. She knew the answer.

Jeff started to open his mouth.

"Jeff," she interrupted. "Whatever hang-ups you have about me or people like me? I have dealt with it all. I have experienced intolerance on a level you can't even begin to fathom."

Jeff started to feel very small. Andrea didn't care about his feelings on the subject.

"Let me do my job. The job your father wants me to do. The job he needs me to do. Because, quite frankly, he can no longer do it on his own. And you can't do it alone. We won't have any problems if you'll just let me do what I need to do."

Andrea seemed to be waiting. She wanted to hear what he had to say. He wanted to yell at her. He wanted to scream at her.

But he had nothing. Just hate and fear. Jeff knew those feelings were not going to win him any arguments.

"Well, since it seems like we are done here, let me leave you with this final thought. If you're going to hate me or people like me, have a valid reason. Hate me because of how I take care of your father. Hate me for not doing my job. Don't hate me for the lifestyle I've chosen because— and I want your little teenage mind to think about this—it is really no different than yours."

And with that Andrea walked down the hallway.

As he watched her go, he was furious. He'd let his big chance to tell Andrea off slip away. Sadly, he knew it didn't matter. He still didn't have anything to say to her.

Chapter 31

DIFFERENT FOR GUYS

How come you dissed Danielle so hard?" Brian asked Jeff over video chat. They were in the middle of their chemistry homework.

"I figured I'd get her before she got me." Jeff acted like he was looking through the chemistry book. "I thought she'd have moved on to somebody else by now."

"So she's had a bunch of boyfriends. She hasn't slept with them all."

"Just most of them." Jeff smiled. Brian didn't.

"If she were a guy, we'd be stoked that he was hooking up with all these people."

"You go out with her."

"She likes you, loser," Brian said.

"Yeah, for now. I don't want to be another hookup."

"You don't know if that's what she wants. All you've done is be weird to her."

Weird?

Jeff bristled at that comment. He wanted to tell Brian to deal with all the pressures of a sick dad *and* school and see if that didn't make him act "weird" too.

"She told me your dad is doing better. How come you didn't tell me?"

"I don't know." Jeff didn't want to talk about his dad. He didn't want to tell Brian about Andrea. He'd probably laugh at him for having somebody like her come to his house. For needing help from her.

"Well, Danielle isn't so bad. She's changed a lot. If I thought she was into me, I'd give it a shot," Brian said.

Chapter 32

COMING HOME, PART 1

Jeff came to Building Up after school to pick up his dad. He was sitting in a wheelchair in his room when he got there. Jeff figured he had to be wheeled to the car, like at the hospital.

"Don't forget my iPad charger," Jeff's dad said.

"I already packed it." Jeff was organizing all of his dad's things. He had brought over more clothes and books when they both realized the stay at Building Up would not be short.

The requests continued.

"Did you get my reading glasses?"

"Where's my book?"

"Where'd you park the car? We need to bring it around. Jeff, we need to bring the car around when they wheel me out."

"Can you stop!" Jeff yelled.

His dad looked at him.

Mr. Song, propped up in bed as daytime TV played in the background, looked at Jeff too.

Jeff felt himself getting sad. He was embarrassed. More than anything, he felt bad for his dad. He could feel tears welling up.

"I'm gonna get the car," he mumbled. "I'll get your stuff when I come back." He walked out of the room.

As Jeff went and got the car, he shifted from feeling sad to terrified. His dad was really coming home. He knew he should've been happy. Instead, he felt like his small world was only getting smaller.

Chapter 33

HOLDING STEADY

Building Up had given his dad a walker. But Jeff's dad didn't use it to get inside the house. Jeff offered to get it out of the trunk. When his dad said no, Jeff didn't want to push it. He wanted his dad to be as independent as he could be.

As soon as he got inside, his dad sat down in his chair in the living room. He turned on the TV. He picked up the phone.

As Jeff began to unpack, his dad started to call people and let them know he was back home.

By the time he was done, his dad was in his bedroom, napping.

Chapter 34

HERE TO STAY

Jeff worked really hard to get all of his homework done. Since his dad was home, he felt he had to be ready for any surprises.

After homework, he video chatted with some kids in the Key Club. They were setting up a food drive for Thanksgiving. It would be at the high school.

He walked downstairs to see how his dad was doing.

"You want to go to dinner?" Jeff's dad asked. He was sitting in his chair again. The evening news was on.

"You feel up to it?" Jeff was surprised.

"Sure." Jeff's dad smiled.

They went to Applebee's. It was one of those places they ate at a few times every month.

Jeff brought the walker from Building Up. He put it in the trunk of the car. His dad didn't feel like using it.

In fact, his dad was getting around well. He wasn't shaking nearly as much. He was moving faster. They walked right into the restaurant and were immediately seated. Jeff didn't even have to wait for his dad to join him at the table.

Jeff knew this was one hundred percent because of Andrea. He knew whatever hang-ups he had about her, she got results. His dad looked good. He was almost moving around and looking as good as he did when Jeff's mom was alive.

"Maybe we don't need Andrea to come." Jeff watched his father.

His dad was eating a steak. Jeff knew it probably wasn't the best thing, but this was his first meal out since being hospitalized.

"The doctor at Building Up thinks we need her help," he said.

He felt his stomach tightening. His dad didn't get it. He was accepting everything too easily. He was accepting Andrea.

"Doesn't she bother you? Nagging you all the time. Talking in that big, pompous voice." Jeff wanted to say a lot more. He wanted to say he thought Andrea was gross. That she wasn't fooling anybody. That she was weird.

"Why do you care? She's helping me. I like her. I think I'm doing a lot better. You even commented on that in the car."

Jeff's dad was right. He'd been happy with how well his dad was doing. Jeff regretted saying that now.

Maybe I don't hate Andrea. Maybe I hate what she represents, he thought.

Her presence was a sign of how sick Jeff's dad was.

Jeff wanted to tell his father to work harder. To try harder to be independent. To not be so needy of help.

As Jeff ate his hamburger, his anger continued to grow. He'd honestly believed his dad could be how he was before he got Parkinson's and heart disease.

These thoughts made him so angry he stopped talking.

His dad didn't seem to notice, and that made Jeff angrier.

REALITY

Nothing about Jeff's day had been easy.

He was up late because he was preparing Key Club information for some local businesses. Jeff overslept and knew he wouldn't make it to school on time. Since his dad was back, he was leaving the car home. Jeff wanted it to be available in case his dad wanted to use it. This meant Jeff had to walk to school.

By the time he got there, he was really late.

Jeff was exhausted by lunch. And he couldn't go home when school was over. He had a meeting with Mr. McDonald. The teacher wanted to see Jeff's proposals to the local businesses. Mr. McDonald liked them, but he wanted to make some revisions.

More work.

As Jeff walked into his house after a long day at school,

he heard Andrea's voice. She was sitting with Jeff's dad watching *Wheel of Fortune*. She was also highlighting some things on a piece of paper.

On the wall in the kitchen was a large whiteboard. It was for Jeff's dad. It listed out his bathing, medication, shopping, and doctors appointments. It noted his schedule for the next month. With the exception of weekends, Andrea had his days covered.

On top of that, Andrea was going to cook meals specifically for his dad's diet. They were all low sodium, low cholesterol, low everything. Andrea made a lot of food so Jeff could eat it too, if he wanted to.

"We're going to talk to your doctor about taking you off some of these medications." Andrea didn't look up from what she was doing.

She had said hi when Jeff walked in. That was the only time she had looked at him.

"You don't think I need all of them?" Jeff's dad's eyes were glued to the TV screen. He was holding a glass of water.

"You probably don't need more than half. Some of them even cancel each other out."

Jeff just stood there. He realized he wasn't needed right now. He figured he could speak to his dad later. Without saying anything, he went up to his room.

As he moved up the stairs, he could still hear Andrea and his dad talking. Jeff slowed his pace. He wanted to know if they were talking about him. If Andrea was saying anything negative.

"Oh, crap!" Jeff's dad said.

"Oh, no worries," Andrea said. "I spill things all the time."

"I just shake like that sometimes." His dad sounded embarrassed.

Jeff realized his dad had spilled something. His Parkinson's had caused it. He sighed and went to his room.

Chapter 36

ALONE WITH HIS THOUGHTS

Jeff knew he should have been reviewing for his tests. But he couldn't.

He was starving. The kitchen was less than thirty steps away. He didn't want to go there. He wanted to wait until Andrea was gone. Until then, he was a prisoner in his own house.

Jeff just lay in his bed, staring at the ceiling. He had gone from thinking about food to thinking about his dad.

More importantly, he was thinking about his own free time. Like right now. Jeff wondered if this was how it would feel when his father was no longer around.

Empty.

Confusing.

Lonely.

Jeff hated thinking like this. He couldn't help it. It

seemed like all his thoughts were negative. In some way he thought that held back his deepest fears. But he knew eventually something bad was going to happen to his dad again. When it did, he would be ready. He would be more involved than last time.

Chapter 37

KEY CLUB

Jeff sat in the Key Club meeting trying to focus. He found if he wasn't thinking about his dad, he was thinking about schoolwork. If he wasn't thinking about that, he was thinking about his future.

There were about ten people in the club. The topic of today's meeting was the Thanksgiving food drive. The Key Club was doing the drive in conjunction with an agency called Give Back. They would see that all the food went where it was supposed to go.

"I cannot tell you how vital your work is to the community," Mr. Marcigliano, the CEO of Give Back, said. "You work so hard all the time. You're so selfless in your giving. I am truly humbled."

Jeff heard his words, but he didn't hear them.

God, I don't feel selfless at all. My dad is a burden. I want him to not be sick. I don't want to take care of him.

Mr. Marcigliano continued talking. Then he said something that got Jeff's attention.

"I always say, no matter how bad you think things are, if everybody in this room put their problems on the table, you'd take yours back."

I don't think that's true at all. I wouldn't wish this on anyone.

Chapter 38

DANIELLE AGAIN

Lunch was almost over. Jeff was thinking about his workload after school. He planned to go to the library and finish his homework. Before Andrea started coming to the house, he would've gone home.

As he walked, he passed Danielle. They made eye contact. Jeff stared briefly into her eyes.

"I'm sorry," he said.

Danielle walked over to him. She was wearing a blue-and-white sundress. Her thick hair was effortlessly perfect.

"How are you?" she asked, walking with him now.

"Okay. You?" He didn't know why he was talking to her. Other than he really wanted to.

"How's your dad?"

Jeff liked the way she asked that. Like they were a team.

"He's doing okay. Getting around well. He still shakes and sleeps a lot from Parkinson's."

"My grandpa had that too. It sucks. I'm sorry you have to deal with it."

Jeff looked at her. She was looking back at him. There was no devilish smile. He liked that. He liked everything about Danielle right now.

"He lived a long time with it. He was ninety-four when he died. It was such a shock losing him." Danielle looked ahead. It was like she was thinking about her grandfather. Like she was remembering everything.

The bell rang.

"Well, good talking with you. Bye, Jeff." Danielle smiled and walked away.

Jeff watched her go.

As good as she had made him feel for those moments, he was bummed again. Not because she was gone.

Jeff's dad was sixty-five. There was no way he would live till ninety-four.

Jeff would've given anything to have his dad live to an age even close to that.

Chapter 39

HOME CONFRONTATION

Jeff misjudged the time and came home too early.

"Sit down. You're always so busy." Jeff's dad laughed.

He and Andrea were watching the news. His dad seemed oblivious to the fact that she made Jeff uncomfortable. He figured Andrea hadn't said anything.

Her shift was supposed to be done. Andrea often hung around, chatting with Jeff's dad for a few minutes at the end of her day. Tonight, she was there longer.

"How was your day?" Andrea asked.

"Good." Jeff glanced at her.

"See that?" Jeff's dad pointed the remote toward the screen. "They are saying gay marriage is gonna be the law of the land."

They were watching CNN. Jeff didn't look at the screen. He didn't say anything. He wanted to go upstairs.

I don't care if people are gay. I don't care if people like Andrea want to be how they are. Whatever. I just don't want to deal with it in my house. Why is that so hard to get? he thought.

"That'll be great for a lot of people, right?" Jeff's dad locked eyes with Andrea.

"Yes, it will." Andrea's tone was even.

"Once people see they have nothing to worry about. Once they see all the tax benefits of recognizing these people. You might be able to start your hormone thing again." Jeff's dad smiled at Andrea.

"Dad." Jeff glared at his father.

"What?" his dad shot back.

Jeff stared at him. He hated how Parkinson's and everything else that was wrong with him seemed to have robbed him of a social filter.

"Does this make you uncomfortable, Jeff?" Andrea smiled. "Your father and I talk about it all the time. Laws like this could be great for me. Right now I can't afford hormone therapy. Forget about facial and breast augmentation."

Jeff was speechless. He didn't understand why Andrea was talking so openly. Why it was okay for her to come to his house and gang up on him with his dad on her side. Why she had to put how she was in his face.

"Do you even know what those procedures are?" Andrea asked. She didn't seem mad. She just seemed like she wasn't going to back down because who she was made Jeff uncomfortable.

He felt his stomach and chest getting tight. Jeff wanted to scream.

"I have an A in English. I know what those words mean." Tony Munigi came to Jeff's mind after he said that. He wondered if he would have those kinds of procedures.

"Maybe if I could afford those kinds of procedures, I might make you more comfortable."

"What?"

"I'd look more like a woman," Andrea said. "I wouldn't look like some hybrid freak."

"I never called you that."

"You don't have to."

Jeff hated Andrea right then. It had nothing to do with what or who she was. He just thought she was being rude.

"What makes you think you can come into my house and talk to me like this?" Jeff's tone was loud, but he wasn't yelling. "You're a new person in my dad's life. I'm his son."

Jeff wanted to say more, but he was so upset he could feel himself starting to cry.

"I may be a new person in your life." Andrea's tone was still even. She wasn't rattled at all. "I am sorry if you feel I've been glib. However, you should know that what I am is not new. It's been around since forever. And it's because of laws and people like your father that I can be more open now. I'm sorry if it bothers you, but that's how it is."

Nobody said anything after that. They went back to watching the news. Eventually, Jeff went upstairs. He had homework to do.

Chapter 40

EMOJI

You guys need to clean that bathroom," Cliff declared as he walked out into the living room. "You don't want it looking like that if you're having people over."

Jeff's dad put on his jacket. He and Cliff were going shopping.

Jeff didn't know what about Cliff's comments bothered him more. Was Cliff too blunt? Or was he pissed off that they never had anybody over? That he didn't invite people over because his house was usually a mess. Or was he embarrassed about people seeing his dad shake and tremble when his meds weren't working?

"There's some Comet under the kitchen sink," Jeff's dad said.

"Okay," Jeff said.

Cliff continued to talk. Jeff's dad listened and they left.

Jeff didn't think the toilet was too gross. Still, he swirled the cleanser around and scrubbed the bowl as much as he could.

He was not happy. It was Saturday. He didn't want to be stuck at home working on Key Club stuff. He didn't want to be cleaning. He didn't want to do homework. Jeff was tired of always trying to get ahead so he could be there for his dad.

Then he remembered that Andrea was taking care of most daily routines. Jeff just had to pick up the slack on the weekends.

This made him even angrier. He had put off having a life for his dad for so long, now there was nothing really holding him back, but he was still miserable.

His phone chimed with a text.

It was Danielle. "I'm bored."

Jeff was tempted to write, "I'm cleaning a toilet."

He didn't.

"Doing homework," Jeff replied.

"I'm coming over." Danielle added an emoji. It was a face. It seemed to be asking, *I'm coming over if you'll let me.*

His first instinct was to say no. Jeff wanted to say he was too busy.

"Okay," he texted back.

Chapter 41

STEPPING IT UP

Where's your dad?" Danielle was sitting about four inches away from him on the couch.

"Out with a friend." Jeff took a sip of his water. Danielle was drinking bottled water she'd brought over.

She was wearing an oversized tan sweatshirt and jeans. It was the middle of October. Jeff always thought Danielle dressed great when the weather changed.

They were watching the '80s show, *Saved By the Bell*.

"He has a caregiver now." Jeff didn't know why he blurted that out. He just did.

"Oh, that's good." Danielle turned and looked at him. Jeff knew he had her full attention. He liked it. "Is the caregiver good?"

"She does a lot of stuff for him. She keeps his meds

organized. Takes him to appointments. She cooks ..." As Jeff recited everything Andrea did, he realized just how much she had changed his life.

"She sounds awesome."

"Yeah." Jeff smiled. "But *she* was a *he* at one point. Her name is Andrea. It probably used to be Andrew or something."

He knew he probably shouldn't have said that. But he wanted to.

"Did she tell you that?" Danielle asked.

"She doesn't have to."

"Does it bother you?"

"Kind of. I don't know. It's just weird having somebody like that in my house."

They stared at each another.

"You do all this community outreach." Danielle smiled. "You help all these people who need help. I've seen you at school doing it. You treat everybody with respect. Doesn't Andrea deserve the same respect?"

"Yeah, it's just—"

"I mean, if your dad is getting great care, and it sounds like he is, why does it matter what she is?"

Jeff stared at Danielle. He suddenly felt overcome. He knew she liked him. He wanted her to like him more. He no longer cared about her past. Jeff just wanted to be even more connected to this girl who hadn't given up on him.

They started to kiss. It was instantly passionate and perfect. Before Jeff knew it, he had scooped her into his lap. They wrapped their arms around one another.

Then the front door opened.

They sprang to their feet.

Jeff's dad and Cliff walked in. After a brief introduction, Jeff told them he and Danielle were going to get something to eat.

As Jeff led Danielle out of the house, he eyed his dad and Cliff. He could tell by the stunned looks on both their faces they thought he had done pretty darn well for himself.

Considering Danielle was the first girl Jeff had ever brought home, he was feeling pretty good too. And for the first time in a long time.

Chapter 42

COUPLE

Jeff and Danielle, without putting a label on their relationship, had become a couple. They talked, texted, and video chatted in some way every day. Over the past few weeks, they had seen each other after school, and on Friday evenings, Saturdays, and sometimes Sundays.

Jeff loved it. He told Danielle everything. How he had always liked her. How he had always wished she would like him. Danielle didn't seem to know any of this. When Jeff asked her why she liked him now, she simply said, "I just saw you one day over the summer at the mall. And it clicked. You didn't even see me. I just thought you were so cute walking around and helping your dad."

Jeff didn't even remember when he had taken his dad to the mall.

BREAKDOWN

So the doctor said everything looks good with your father's cholesterol and blood pressure." Andrea had intercepted Jeff in the driveway that evening.

He'd stayed late at school. The Key Club was making banners for the upcoming food drive. Danielle had helped.

"Now they want to up some of his Parkinson's medications because of the shaking, but your dad and I are against it. Especially if it is going to make him more tired."

As Andrea spoke, Jeff saw Mr. Miles, a neighbor, behind them. He was working on his car. Mr. Miles had hung a light so he could see his work. Every so often he looked up at them.

Jeff could tell he was staring at Andrea.

"The only other concern I have is your father mentioned being dizzy."

Jeff stared at Andrea. If she could tell Jeff was concerned about the neighbor seeing her, she didn't show it. He figured she probably didn't care. Jeff wished he could be like that.

"Has he mentioned that to you?" she went on.

Jeff shook his head.

He wanted this conversation to be over. Andrea could be here with his dad when Jeff wasn't home. His dad could tell him what was going on. Nobody in the neighborhood needed to know about Andrea.

"Keep an eye on that. Your dad might not share that with you." Andrea put her hand on Jeff's shoulder. Her masculine-looking hand. A hand she would probably change if she could afford it. "Sometimes parents can't stop being parents long enough to see that their children are no longer kids."

Again, Jeff nodded his head. He watched the neighbor. Even though it was starting to get dark, he thought he saw him laugh. Laughing at the crisis Jeff's family was in.

"Okay." Andrea's tone changed, and this got Jeff's attention. "I can see you don't want to talk about this or anything related to me."

"No, it's not that," Jeff said meekly. Andrea was really good at making her points. She could defend herself in a way Jeff could not.

"I know you don't want your dad to be sick. But do you

think I really want to work in a home where the son of a patient I care about hates me? Can't you get past yourself for a minute and see I might actually be good for your father?"

Their eyes were locked in confrontation. This was hard for Jeff.

"I don't hate you," he finally said.

"Then what is it?"

"I don't understand—"

"You don't understand?" Andrea interrupted. "Well, let me help you."

"I don't understand any of this. Why any of this stuff has happened. To my dad and to me."

Andrea's face dropped slightly. Any bit of anger she had was gone.

Jeff felt himself starting to cry. He quickly turned and walked away from Andrea.

He went inside and shut the door. Jeff didn't even say hi to his dad. He just went into his room and sobbed into his pillow.

He didn't want his dad to hear him. And he really didn't want Andrea to follow him inside.

Chapter 44

NOT MY DAD

After school a few days later, Jeff and some friends went to a supermarket after school. It was close to campus. There was going to be a bake sale to benefit the school, and they needed to buy cookie and brownie mix. The Key Club had gotten permission to make the baked goods at school.

Even though Jeff had been in the Key Club with his friends since freshman year, he didn't really know them.

As they walked through the store, Jeff wandered away to find parchment paper. When he passed the frozen section, he saw his dad and Andrea.

They were at the far end of the frozen foods, near the organic section. Both of them had their backs turned to Jeff.

Jeff noticed that Andrea really looked like a woman from behind.

He also noticed how much his dad was shaking. How

slow his movements were. It seemed to take him forever to put something back in the case.

Jeff wondered if his dad's Parkinson's meds should be increased.

Andrea was helping him. She was close, in case Jeff's dad needed anything. In case he fell or something like that. She had said she wanted him to be more independent.

Jeff couldn't stop staring at his dad. He looked so old. Anybody looking at him would think he was a lot older than his mid-sixties.

Jeff knew he should've gone over and said hi.

But he didn't.

He texted his friends that something had come up, and he'd meet them back at school.

Chapter 45

PRESENT FUTURE

Principal Burnette's office was nice. The walls were lined with awards, letters, and educational credentials he had worked for. There were also pictures of his family on the wall and on his desk.

He was tall, with a thick head of graying blond hair. Principal Burnette was smiling at Jeff.

"I want to involve the whole community in this year's Thanksgiving drive." Whenever Principal Burnette spoke, his eyes got big. It was like he wanted Jeff to know how serious he was.

"Okay, not a problem." Jeff started thinking about contacting more businesses and putting signs in places people would see them.

"This time of year, the spirit of giving is really present. We need to capitalize on it."

They talked a little more about ways they could do this.

"People like you do things." Principal Burnette smiled at him. "You make me jealous, Jeff. You have your whole life ahead of you to make a difference."

"Thank you, sir. You seem like you've certainly done that with yours." Jeff hoped he didn't sound like a suck-up. However, it wasn't every day the principal of the school complimented him.

"High test scores are no longer enough. I'm telling you, Jeff, you're the kind of student colleges are fighting over now because of your skill set. Because of how much you care about helping the community."

As Jeff walked through school, he didn't feel right. Things were going too well.

His dad, despite Parkinson's, was doing okay.

Danielle was into him.

He was up on his schoolwork and club commitments.

What about the future?

What if I did do something great?

Would Dad be around to see it?

Jeff told himself to not think about this. He told himself to be happy. He felt like he deserved to be.

He thought about Andrea. She was part of the community, wasn't she?

What was Jeff doing for her?

Chapter 46

BUILDING

Danielle came over after school. In between make-out sessions in Jeff's bedroom, they actually tried to get their homework done. They had set up their work so they were across from one another on the floor. At a moment's notice, they could instantly lock lips.

Jeff was slowly admitting that he was in Danielle's world. He loved it.

Danielle accepted him. Even better, she made Jeff feel normal. He didn't feel like the other shoe was about to drop with his dad anymore.

He figured that everything felt very natural with Danielle because this was what he had wanted for so long. The two of them had even talked about their relationship as being "meant to be."

They hadn't had sex yet. Jeff knew it certainly was a

possibility. He had never looked at girls this way. Whenever he and his friends talked about them, he was always the person not saying anything.

Before Danielle, there had been times when Jeff even wondered if he were gay. He didn't think about it too much. Jeff always liked girls. But he didn't—or couldn't—do anything about it. Being around Andrea had made Jeff wonder about this part of his identity. Maybe this was another reason why he felt uncomfortable around her. But that wasn't Andrea's fault and he knew it.

They were staring at each other as "Same in the End," by Sublime, played on Pandora. Danielle had set it on her iPhone and put the speaker on.

"How much more do you have?" she asked.

"English and then some pre-calculus. You?"

"I'm almost done with history." Danielle held up her paper.

They heard the front door open. They heard Jeff's dad's voice.

Then Jeff heard Andrea. His face dropped. He was sure Danielle saw it.

"Is that her?" Danielle wasn't saying it rudely. Jeff could see she really wanted to know.

"Yeah."

Danielle stood up. She took his hand.

"Let's go downstairs and say hi."

"Why?" Jeff asked as he stood up involuntarily.

"Why not?" She gave him a quick kiss. She then gave him a long stare with her hypnotic eyes. They weren't devilish anymore, but encouraging. "Everything's going to be fine."

Jeff believed her.

Chapter 47

DINNER GUESTS

The quick hello had turned into Danielle staying for dinner. Andrea was going to cook for Jeff's dad. But one thing led to another and they were all eating together.

To Jeff's surprise, he was really enjoying himself. They were all talking and laughing. It reminded Jeff of how things had been when his mother was alive.

"If you two have known each other for so long"—Jeff's dad took a bite of the gluten-free pasta Andrea had made— "why am I just meeting you now?"

Danielle looked at Jeff with a big smile on her face. Her eyes were glowing.

"Jeff ignored me." She and Andrea exchanged a glance and laughed.

"Yeah." Jeff smiled. "It wasn't me ignoring her. I can assure you of that."

"You didn't ignore me?" Danielle playfully kicked him under the table. Jeff loved it.

"That sounds like my first crush: Alejandra Mendez," Andrea said.

Jeff looked down at the table. He didn't know where Andrea was going with this. Danielle didn't say anything.

"You liked a girl?" Jeff's dad asked innocently. He really didn't seem to notice what Andrea was. He also didn't seem to realize his question might be insensitive.

"Yes, William." Andrea patted him on the shoulder and laughed. "I wasn't born this way."

Danielle cracked up. Jeff's dad laughed.

And Jeff smiled despite himself.

NEW NORMAL ACCEPTED

A week or so later, Jeff came home right after school. He didn't even think about Andrea being there.

He walked in, and his dad was nodding off in front of the TV. A commercial about reverse mortgages was airing.

Andrea was in the kitchen making dinner.

"Hey," Jeff said.

"Hello." Andrea smiled.

They made eye contact. Sometimes it was impossible to ignore that Andrea was once a man. Her features were very masculine. It made Jeff turn away.

He was always worried that one day he'd stare for too long. Jeff worried that if he did, Andrea would call him out. He was scared that this sweet and loving person would become mean and awful.

"How's Danielle?" Andrea asked.

"Good. I actually need to text her. She wanted to do something later."

"Can I tell you something?" Andrea asked.

"Sure."

"She really likes you."

"Did she tell you that?"

"She didn't have to. You can just feel a person's energy sometimes. It's like she's drawn to you."

"Oh, thanks." Jeff smiled.

He felt weird talking about this. Not because of what Andrea was. Jeff just felt weird talking about himself like this.

"Why wouldn't she like you?" Andrea went on. "You're such a good person, Jeff. Look at how devoted you are to your father. All the charity work you do. You've got a full plate, and you really handle it well."

Jeff felt his body tense up. Tears were forming in his eyes.

He was always so busy thinking about what was ahead. He rarely thought about himself in the here and now.

"Thanks again. I gotta do some homework."

He walked away, thinking about how he felt like a jerk. He hadn't meant to be rude. Jeff just wasn't ready to share his feelings with Andrea.

BEING GUYS

Dude," Daryl joked. "Girls have it so much easier than guys. All they have to do is go up to a guy and say 'let's mack out,' and it's on."

"Well, the guy has to want to bone the girl." Brian laughed.

Jeff was listening. He had always been quiet whenever people talked about girls. Now that he and Danielle were together, he knew he could talk about her. But he didn't want to. What went on between them wasn't only private. It was special. He didn't want to talk about it just to be one of the guys.

He couldn't help but think about Andrea too. She was a woman, but she hadn't always been that way. Was it easier for her now? Did she even want to be with guys?

Danielle said she thought Andrea still wanted to be with

women. Jeff didn't think Andrea being a woman now made it any easier.

He wanted to tell his friends that but he didn't.

"Hey, Jeff, what did you do to Danielle?" Daryl smiled.

"Do to her?" Jeff got a sinking feeling. Had she been talking? Had she been telling people about him? About what he was like?

"He means that in a good way," Brian said.

"Oh yeah, for sure," Daryl said. "Nobody's ever seen her so sprung on a dude. Chris Lohman tried to hook up with her again, and she flat-out denied him. She said it was because of you."

Chris Lohman had graduated two years ago. He had been the first guy to have sex with Danielle. Jeff had seen them hanging out a lot. She looked at Chris then the same way she looked at Jeff now. Chris ended up cheating on her, and they broke up.

Jeff couldn't help but smile. Danielle kept proving him wrong. She wasn't who he thought she was at all.

And Jeff was realizing the same thing about Andrea.

LEAK

Jeff was sitting at the kitchen table. He was brainstorming ideas to present to the Key Club for the Christmas fundraiser. The Thanksgiving one hadn't happened yet. Jeff wanted to get ahead. He wanted to show Mr. McDonald and Principal Burnette that he was every bit the model student they thought he was.

Jeff's dad and Andrea walked in. They both had wary looks on their faces.

"Uh, Jeff," his dad started. "You need to take me to the hospital in a few hours. They did a chest x-ray and found some fluid in my lungs."

"I would do it," Andrea said as she went in the kitchen to make dinner. "But I've gotta take my own dad to an appointment."

Jeff's dad sat down in front of the TV. He pressed the power button on the remote. A *Gunsmoke* rerun came on.

As Jeff reviewed his Christmas fundraiser ideas, he had a thought. It didn't matter how ahead he got. His dad was sick, and Jeff could never get out of the way of his illness.

Chapter 51

WRONG

Dr. Wilson, his dad's main doctor, smiled slightly as he examined his father's recent chest x-ray.

"Your lungs have fluid," he said, looking at Jeff first and then his father.

Jeff's dad didn't react in any way.

"Okay. So can you drain it?" Jeff asked.

"We can," Dr. Wilson said, staring at the x-ray. "But then we'll just have drain it again."

Dr. Wilson turned and started typing on his computer.

Jeff's dad stared at the ground. Jeff could tell by the way he was looking that he knew what was going on.

Jeff got nervous fast. He wished Andrea were here. He knew she was better at being in charge of his father than he was.

Chapter 52

BACK IN THE WRONG SADDLE

Well, they've admitted me." Jeff's dad was in a hospital bed again. He was talking on the phone to Cliff. "I don't know if it's cancer. But they said the labs came back on the blood. Something doesn't look right." He looked at Jeff after he said that.

Jeff was leaning against the wall. He wanted to disappear into it.

More than anything, he didn't want to be back here with his dad.

"Okay, Cliff," his dad said. "Yeah, I will. Bye."

"Hello," a pleasant voice said right as Jeff's dad hung up the phone.

Dr. Naphtali walked into the room. He was dressed in surgical scrubs. He was clean-shaven. Not one hair was out of place. His hands were big and manicured.

"I'm going to be the surgeon performing your lung biopsy, Mr. Corman." Dr. Naphtali shook Jeff's dad's hand. Then he shook Jeff's. "Then I will drain the fluid."

Biopsy? Jeff was baffled.

"That means I want to take out a small piece and send it to the lab," the doctor explained.

How does a leak in Dad's lung mean that he has cancer? he thought.

But he didn't ask. He figured he'd Google it later.

He looked at his dad. He was staring through Dr. Naphtali.

"What if I don't do it?" Jeff's dad finally asked.

This made Jeff feel better. Maybe there was another way.

"What are your options? Are you going to come here and have your lungs drained every few days? Or every day? And your labs make me suspect something else is going on. We do this surgery. If the fluid is the only problem, we can stop it."

Jeff suddenly felt a mix of sadness and anger.

I am an idiot. I actually thought I could have a normal life. I actually thought I could be a normal high school teenager with a girlfriend.

Jeff had been so happy these past few weeks. Then he realized maybe he was being punished for being that way.

Chapter 53

NEXT MORNING

Danielle wanted to skip school, but Jeff told her not to. She did insist on coming by the hospital after Jeff's dad's surgery.

The morning had been a whirlwind. It seemed like the second Jeff showed up, they wheeled his dad into surgery. Andrea was there too. They stopped them in the hall before the elevator. Jeff's dad signed some papers. Andrea told him they were legal papers, ensuring that somebody would pay for whatever insurance didn't.

What?! They are giving him these papers now? Why now? That's so cold, he thought. He was starting to get angry again.

After that, they took an elevator downstairs. They waited in a prep room. Before Jeff and his dad could talk, Dr. Naphtali walked in. He was dressed in scrubs still. He explained what he was going to do. And then he ended with, "And if it is cancer, we will refer you to an oncologist, who will start you on chemo."

It was so impersonal.

Jeff hated all of it.

Chapter 54

WAITING ROOM

Jeff and Andrea sat in the waiting room. As he looked around, Jeff noticed the other families there. He wondered if having more people around would make him feel any better. He figured it might. Then he realized it didn't matter. Aside from babies being born, nobody was in the hospital because something good was happening.

"I hate these places too," Andrea said. She had obviously read the look on Jeff's face. "I may have elected to have surgery, but that didn't make coming here any better."

The surgery.

Jeff didn't want to talk about it. He read the sign that said No Cell Phones. Nobody was following that rule.

"What was it like?" Jeff asked. He figured if Andrea was here, they might as well talk about something. He also thought if she talked, then he wouldn't have to talk at all.

"Do you really want to know about my genital surgery?" Andrea asked.

For the first time ever, Jeff realized he wasn't seeing Andrea as anything other than a person at the hospital in a time of crisis. A friend. He didn't notice all the male facial features or her strong hands.

Jeff hadn't even thought about what people might think about them sitting together. Despite knowing that his dad was in bad shape, Jeff realized he was very comfortable with Andrea being there.

"Tell me what you think I can handle." He smiled.

Andrea couldn't help but smile too.

"My real name is Mike Connors."

Jeff's jaw dropped. It hadn't been Andrew. He wasn't even close.

"I can tell by your expression we should probably keep things pretty simple."

"Can you have kids?" Jeff blurted out.

"No." Andrea didn't seem bothered by this question. "There are certain things required, like ovaries and a uterus. You have to be born with the right equipment."

"Oh." Jeff felt like an idiot. He knew anatomy. He wondered if he sounded insensitive. Or dumb.

"Aren't you gonna ask me why?" Andrea smiled.

"Why what?" Jeff knew what Andrea meant.

And Jeff did want to ask Andrea why she would subject

herself to such a brutal transition. Why would she put her body through it?

"Well, while I may not have chosen to be who I am, I could have elected not to have surgery. In fact, for a while I just dressed up. But it reached a point ..." Andrea took a deep breath. "Imagine you've felt imprisoned your whole life. But there's a way out. There's a way for you to be really free. To fully feel who you believe you were meant to be. Is any amount of temporary physical discomfort worth stopping that?"

He thought about asking Andrea if she wanted to be with men or women. He decided not to. It didn't matter.

Andrea was free.

AFTERMATH

Υou look good, Dad," Jeff said to his father.

It was an hour after the surgery. He was propped up in his hospital bed. The machines were still monitoring him. His hair was messy.

There was another machine. A tube was connected to Jeff's dad and the machine. It was draining his lung. A container was filling up with purple liquid that looked like Kool-Aid.

Jeff wanted to know why his dad's lungs were still being drained.

"You'll be back running around in no time," Andrea said.

"I feel all right," Jeff's dad replied.

"I'd better get back to Building Up. I'll visit again tomorrow," Andrea said. "Jeff, call me when you know what room he's in."

Jeff's dad was in a recovery room now. They were going to move him to a regular room soon.

"Sure. Thanks for coming," Jeff said.

They stared at each other. Jeff felt good. He felt like they were friends now. He felt like Andrea knew it too.

"No need to thank me. I wouldn't have missed it."

Andrea left.

"We owe her," Jeff's father said. "Big-time."

Jeff agreed completely.

Chapter 56

MORPHINE

Danielle texted Jeff, but he didn't respond. They had talked at school. Jeff had shown up at fourth period. He was glad his homework tonight was light.

Danielle had wanted to come to the hospital. Jeff told her tomorrow would be better. She texted him, asking why. Jeff didn't have an answer. So he didn't respond. He felt bad holding Danielle at arm's length from his life. He hadn't been doing that recently. But for some reason he felt like he had to now.

Then he saw his dad, and he was glad he'd told her not to come.

His father was trying to eat, but he couldn't. He kept dropping his utensils. Then he tried to sip his water and spilled it all over his food tray. Eventually, his dad started picking at his food with his fingers.

"You want me to cut it up and feed it to you?" Jeff asked. He wanted to ask sooner, but he was having a hard time processing what he was seeing.

"No, Lenny," his dad responded.

"Lenny?"

Jeff's dad stared blankly at him.

"Dad, I'm not Uncle Lenny."

Jeff's father laughed. And laughed.

Jeff wanted to take out his phone. He wanted to record his father so he could show it to him later. Maybe they could laugh about it together.

But he didn't.

Eventually a nurse came in.

"You're father just smashed his food with his fingers?" she asked.

"Yeah, he's really out of it."

"It's the morphine," she said. "For his pain."

Jeff stared at his dad.

He stayed at the hospital for a while. His dad continued to call him Lenny. Then he said he was tired. Jeff seized the moment and left.

Danielle texted him, "Want me to come over later?"

Again, Jeff didn't respond.

Chapter 57

ANOTHER SLEEPLESS NIGHT

If it is cancer," Cliff had said after Jeff told him how his dad was acting earlier. "Maybe it's eating his brain."

Jeff couldn't stop thinking about that comment. He was resting on the couch downstairs. It was dark. The TV was off. After watching so much of it at the hospital and at Building Up, Jeff didn't care if he watched TV ever again.

Cliff had talked about Jeff being more involved. Again. About how Jeff might have to participate in making decisions for his dad.

Jeff wanted to believe his father's behavior was because of the painkillers. Something told him it wasn't.

Chapter 58

WHAT HE BELIEVES

I tell you, that was some presentation last night," Jeff's dad said.

"What?"

Jeff had visited his dad before school. He didn't look any better. His hair was still a mess. But at least he was in a regular room now.

"These guys," his dad giggled. "They wheeled me to the lobby. And this guy—oh man—he made a presentation about the hospital."

"They wheeled you out of your hospital room?" This didn't sound right. "Are you sure you didn't dream it, Dad?"

"It seemed real."

Jeff stared at his dad. Again, he told himself it was the meds.

"Hello," Dr. Wilson said as he walked in. "How are you

feeling, William?" Dr. Wilson glanced at Jeff's dad and eyed his chart. It was on a clipboard.

"All right."

"That's great." Dr. Wilson initialed something and put the clipboard down.

"Dr. Wilson," Jeff finally said. "My dad says they gave a presentation about the hospital last night. That they wheeled him out of here—"

"I doubt they did that." He looked at Jeff. Then he looked back at his dad. "Did they really do that, William? Or do you think it was a dream?"

"It was probably a dream."

"Well." Dr. Wilson looked at Jeff. "I checked his chart. Everything looks good. He can go home later today."

Dr. Wilson smiled and walked out of the room.

Jeff looked at his dad. He may have been awake. He may have been lucid, but he didn't look like he could move.

"He's sending you home?" Jeff asked with shock.

"He seems to think I'm ready." Jeff's dad shrugged.

Chapter 59

TIGHTENING

Jeff showed up at school for second period.

He was as scared as he had ever been. He wasn't so much afraid about his dad dying. He was used to his father's medical issues, like his Parkinson's. He was more nervous about what would happen to him before he died.

"HE'S NOT READY TO COME HOME!" he wanted to scream. "HE NEEDS TO STAY IN THE HOSPITAL. HE NEEDS TO REST. HE NEEDS PEOPLE AROUND THAT CAN CARE FOR HIM!"

Sadly, Jeff knew this wasn't what was really bothering him. As much as he loved his dad, he was going to have to give up his life even more for him.

That thought scared him most of all.

Jeff had a quick conversation with Danielle before going to sixth period. She wanted to know how "Dad" was.

She told Jeff she wanted to be there for him. She told him everything he wanted to hear.

But it was hard to listen to any of it.

Eventually, the hospital called. Jeff figured they were calling him to come and get his father. He ducked out of sixth period. It was AP Chemistry and they were doing a lab.

But that wasn't why the hospital was calling. The doctors had assessed his father again.

Jeff's dad was going back to Building Up.

The labs hadn't come back yet. But Jeff knew they would soon.

BACK

I'm nervous," Jeff's dad said in a low whisper.

He was back at Building Up. He was lying down. The TVs were playing. Nurses, patients, and doctors were roaming the halls. It was just like last time.

Except Jeff's dad had a new roommate. This new guy was big. He was a white guy with a long beard. His name was Clay.

The guy looked like a lumberjack. Jeff imagined he'd lived in the mountains his whole life. Then he got sick, and they brought him to Building Up.

"Why are you nervous?" Jeff asked.

His dad was still out of it. Jeff kept waiting for the fog to lift. He kept waiting for the meds to wear off.

"I don't want to pee on this guy's floor."

Jeff stared at his dad. He realized his father didn't know where he was. He thought he was in Clay's house.

"Dad," Jeff whispered. "Clay doesn't own this place. You're at Building Up."

A nurse walked in. "Somebody need to use the bathroom?" she asked.

Jeff got out of the way. The nurse helped his dad stand up with his walker. His dad and the nurse walked into the bathroom.

Chapter 61

MEDS

Jeff sat at the kitchen table. He had made himself some soup but hadn't eaten any of it. It was supposed to be healthy and low in sodium. Jeff wondered how many other teenagers thought about their sodium.

He was looking over a two-page list of medications that Building Up had printed for him.

His dad wasn't on new medications. This was the current list of meds his father always took. The only difference now was that he was on a low-dose painkiller.

After going over the list a few more times, Jeff started to cry. His tears rolled down his cheeks onto the list. He told himself to stop. He knew he had nothing to cry about.

Yet.

His dad was still alive.

But it didn't matter.

Death was coming. Jeff knew it was coming.

His dad could rest all he wanted. He could take all the medications they gave him.

He was still going to die.

There's no saving him, he thought.

There was a knock on the door.

It was Danielle.

She started to cry when she saw him. They stood in the doorway, hugging. Jeff was breathing hard. His heart was pounding so much he was worried he might scare her.

But she didn't let go.

"You're so special, Jeff. You're so great and awesome. I've always known it," she kept whispering in his ear.

"Why can't I help him?" he sobbed. "Why can't I feel good about what I'm doing? Why don't I want to do it?"

Chapter 62

THE OTHER SHOE

Adenocarcinoma," Dr. Naphtali said.

It was the passing period between third and fourth. Jeff had five minutes to talk.

"So …" Jeff took a deep breath. "No cancer."

"No, he has adenocarcinoma. That's lung cancer. When I did the biopsy, I knew it. Unfortunately, it also looks to be stage four, which was another one of my fears."

The doctor didn't sound fearful to Jeff. He almost sounded happy, like he had gotten an answer right on a test.

Dr. Naphtali recommended an oncologist. He talked about doing more tests. It sounded like Jeff's dad was going to spend the rest of his life being poked and prodded.

When he hung up, Jeff didn't know what to do. So he went to class.

GIVING DAD A DEATH SENTENCE

Jeff went to Building Up after class. It was lunchtime.

"I spoke to the surgeon," Jeff said.

His dad was sitting up. He'd eaten about a third of the turkey sandwich he'd been given. They had also shaved his whiskers and combed his hair.

Jeff was hoping Dr. Naphtali had called his dad.

"What'd he say?" Jeff's dad was staring at him. Talking seemed like a lot of work. He was the most present Jeff had seen him since the surgery.

"He says …" Jeff stopped talking. He hated doing it, and it was so hard to say. He was surprised he could tell him at all. This was his dad. His father. "That you have it."

Jeff's dad looked away. He was gone. He didn't have to try to focus any longer.

"I'm here for you, Dad. I love you. I'll help you fight. I'll do everything I can."

He meant those words. As tough as it would be. As hard as all this was and had been. He loved his dad. He wanted to do everything he could.

His dad shook his head. Jeff could see he was in shock. He looked so weak.

His dad had been a good man who loved and took care of his family. But now he could barely do anything for himself.

A TV show played.

His dad's roommate slept.

This would go on and on.

Chapter 64

RUNNING OUT

Jeff was visiting Building Up three times a day. Time passed quickly. His father had already been there for ten days.

Jeff didn't think his dad was improving much. He had gone from moving slowly to not moving much at all.

He told his physical therapists he didn't feel like exercising. Andrea warned Jeff that if his dad said that too much, eventually they would stop coming.

With his dad safe at Building Up, Jeff could continue his life. His relationship with Danielle was good. She wanted to go to Building Up more than Jeff wanted her to.

If Jeff was there and Cliff came to visit at the same time, Jeff would leave. He told himself it was because he didn't want his dad to be so dependent on him. But he knew that wasn't the real reason.

"So, have you thought about what comes after this?" Jeff asked his dad.

He was hoping his dad had thought about it. He hoped he had a plan. Then Jeff could just carry it out. He knew there were a lot of places his dad could go. He just didn't know where to begin. Which places were better. What they could afford. How to apply.

"Yeah." Jeff's dad looked at him for a moment. "I'll go home."

Jeff had a lot more questions. He would've asked them, but he didn't think his dad had the answers.

Chapter 65

DATE NIGHT

You're up." Jeff smiled as he and Danielle walked into his dad's room. They were on their way out to get something to eat. Danielle talked Jeff into stopping by Building Up. He'd planned to do it after their date. But Danielle was very persuasive.

Jeff's dad smiled at them. He was standing up on his own next to the bed.

Jeff felt a spark of excitement. He thought maybe his dad was inspired to fight the cancer now. Maybe he was going to get better.

Clay checked out Danielle from the next bed. He saw Jeff watching him, but he didn't look away. A game show was on television.

"You look good, Mr. Corman," Danielle said. If she thought this situation was awkward, she didn't show it. Jeff really liked that about her.

"I was going to the bathroom," Jeff's dad said.

He moved toward it and almost fell. Jeff moved over and helped him stay upright.

"Call the nurse for help," Jeff said tersely to Danielle.

He wasn't angry at his dad for being out of bed. He was angry because his dad couldn't even stand up without almost falling over.

A nurse came in and took Jeff's dad into the bathroom.

Jeff sat in a chair. Danielle moved over to him. She put her hand on his shoulder. She smelled great. Just being near her was comforting. But it was overwhelming for her to be here. Building Up was depressing.

"You're so tense," she said as she massaged his shoulders.

"Can you blame me?" Jeff snapped.

He glared at her. Then he felt bad and looked away.

"No," she said.

He put his hand on hers. "I'm sorry."

MOUNTING CRISIS

Jeff was in the business office at Building Up, talking to his father's case administrator, Rosa. "Your father cannot be home alone. It could be very dangerous," she said. "He really needs twenty-four hour care."

Jeff wasn't surprised to hear it. In fact, it was a relief to hear that other people knew his dad was too ill to care for himself. They knew Jeff couldn't do it on his own.

"Can Andrea help?" Jeff was starting to relax. If Andrea could be in the house more, it would really help them out. He could still live his life and know his dad was being taken care of properly.

"She can do twenty-five hours a week." Rosa consulted some papers.

Jeff figured that was okay. It would be like how it was before the lung biopsy.

"Based on my coverage notes, she can help for a few weeks once your father leaves this facility."

"And then what?"

"And then his coverage ends."

So once his dad left Building Up, Andrea would only be coming to the house for a little while longer.

"What can I do for my dad?" Jeff wasn't relaxed any longer. He could feel himself becoming tense and scared.

"There are board-and-care facilities." Jeff hated how matter-of-fact Rosa sounded. He figured she had these types of conversations all the time.

"Are they like Building Up?" He just wanted his dad to be cared for.

"They may not have all the amenities we have. They would need to be a hospice facility. Because the goal is to provide comfortable end-of-life care."

End of life.

Jeff hated these words. He hated how death seemed to be a business.

"Have you discussed any of these options with your father?" Rosa asked.

NOWHERE

Dad, we have to talk about this." Jeff was trying to maintain control. He was trying to be calm. He didn't want to upset his father. He didn't want his roommate to eavesdrop. "You need to be somewhere where you'll be safe."

"How do you know I won't be safe at home?" Jeff's dad locked eyes with him for a second. Then he stared at the TV. But he wasn't really paying attention to the program.

"Dad." Jeff gritted his teeth. "Look at you. You can barely move."

"You'll help me." His dad smiled. It was almost like he didn't realize or understand how serious this was.

Doesn't he get it? Doesn't he understand that this is nuts? I can't do this by myself, he thought. "What about school? Taking the SATs? My clubs? My life?" Jeff said out loud, instantly regretting his selfishness.

His dad stared at him.

"What can I tell you, Jeff? This is a crisis."

"Okay." Jeff nodded his head.

He wanted to say more. He wanted his father to see that he couldn't be home around the clock. But Jeff said nothing. He was unable to put the words together. He knew he needed to be content being a soldier in a losing war.

Chapter 68

ENDING AT THE START

Jeff figured the bedroom couldn't have been more than ten by ten. It had a bed and an old TV. This was where Jeff's dad would live out his final days if he moved to this board-and-care facility.

Andrea was standing in the room with him.

"Well, you could make it more like home," Andrea offered. She could tell Jeff didn't like this place.

"He's not going to like this facility. Not when he has a house of his own," Jeff said.

"You're probably right."

"A guy works his whole life. He does all the right things. And his last days are spent in a strange place." Jeff was starting to seethe with anger.

Jasmine, the woman who ran the facility, came in.

"I have a hospice waiver," she said. "We do provide hospice care here when your dad needs it."

Jeff looked at her. He hated how easy this was for people to talk about. How simple and insignificant they all made death seem.

"Have your father come here." Jasmine smiled. "He'll be very happy."

MAZECARE

I think I'm just gonna take my dad home and see how he does," Jeff said.

Andrea was driving. Jeff noticed she had a very concentrated expression as she drove.

He also saw a hint facial hair. He wondered how much work she had to do to be feminine. He wondered if it bothered her. He figured Andrea was happy and probably didn't mind the maintenance by now.

"You can appeal to Medicare." She looked at him. "To keep him at Building Up. I agree with you, Jeff, he's not ready to go home."

"So why would they release him?"

"His Medicare coverage is used up."

"What happens when Medicare gets used up?" Andrea looked at Jeff after he said that. "So that's how this works, huh? Eventually, the money runs out so you can't be around any longer either. Then I'll really be on my own."

He thought he might cry.

"Don't worry about that." Andrea smiled. "I'm here for you guys."

Danielle was great. She gave Jeff support. He needed that. But she was still a teenager too.

Andrea was there for Jeff in a different way. She was right in the trenches. She knew his dad. She knew what he needed. She could keep him safe.

Jeff appreciated her reassurances but it also bothered him. He hated being at the mercy of the healthcare system. He hated being at the mercy of other people.

Even more, he hated knowing about Medicare, rehabilitative facilities, and hospice when his friends were all able to go about their lives, not having a care in the world.

"I'll help you appeal to Medicare," Andrea said. "You should get an answer right away."

Chapter 70

WEEKEND

Your claim for a Medicare extension has been denied," a robotic voice on Jeff's voice mail said. "As a reminder …"

The robotic voice went on to say that Jeff's dad was being discharged that Monday. It noted the discharge time too. Jeff would have to be there to pick up his father. He wouldn't be able to go to school that day.

The voice went on to say he could call if he had any questions. The voice recited the hours available to speak to a live person at Medicare.

It was Saturday afternoon. The person who had spoken to Jeff wasn't there. Probably having a relaxing weekend.

He stopped listening to his voice mail. He hurled his phone against the wall. But it didn't make him feel any better. He quickly picked it up to make sure it still worked. It did.

He sat down on the couch and closed his eyes. Sleep came quickly.

He woke with a start. He could hear someone knocking at the front door. He checked his phone.

He had missed three texts from Danielle.

"Wanna eat?"

"Where are you?"

"I'm coming over!"

Jeff was thankful Danielle couldn't see him sitting on the couch.

He assumed she was at the door. She continued knocking.

Jeff curled up into a ball. He wanted to be as small as possible. To disappear. Danielle continued to text him. Jeff didn't respond. Eventually, she left. He was alone again.

Chapter 71

COMING HOME, PART 2

Jeff and his dad didn't say too much when they drove home from Building Up.

He had missed school that morning. He thought about going in late. He knew he would only be able to do that if his dad was settled and okay.

He wasn't. Jeff had wheeled him to the car. His dad couldn't move from the wheelchair to the passenger seat. Jeff used all of his strength to hoist him into the car. When they got home, Jeff heaved his dad out of the car. Then they walked slowly into the house.

Jeff saw a neighbor across the street. He was mowing his lawn. He was staring at them, but trying to act like he wasn't. Jeff didn't blame him. Why would he help them? Jeff didn't want to be in this situation either.

Once they got inside, Jeff sat his dad in front of the TV

in the living room. He got a pillow. Then he turned on CNN.

"Just like Building Up." His dad smiled.

Jeff started to look over some calculus homework in the kitchen. He told himself he could do this. He could get his work done around his dad. Just like before.

"Jeff," his dad called five minutes later. "Help me to the bathroom."

Jeff did.

"Could you help me unbuckle my belt and get my pants down?"

"Sure," Jeff said. He tried to tell himself this wasn't happening. That his dad wouldn't always be this needy.

After getting his dad situated, Jeff got back to work. It took him a while to remember where he was with his assignment.

"Jeff," his dad called again.

"Yeah?" Jeff called back from the kitchen table.

"I need you to wipe me."

Jeff's heart sank. He felt so bad for his dad. So bad for this horrible situation.

Jeff walked into the bathroom. His dad had turned the other way. His pants were down. Jeff got some toilet paper and cleaned his father.

"Well, I guess I'm paying you back for all the times I did this for you," his dad joked.

Jeff didn't laugh. He didn't say anything.

Chapter 72

ORGANIZATION

He can't stay here," Cliff said.

They were in Jeff's dad's bedroom. His dad was lying on the bed, watching a small TV. Jeff had helped him get there from the bathroom. He knew the only reason he had managed was because his dad was already standing. Once he sat or lay down, it was almost impossible for Jeff to get him up by himself.

A fan was blowing in the room. It was a few feet from the bed. Aside from a bureau, there was also a small couch in the room. They had been planning to get rid of it over the summer. It never happened.

"I know," Jeff said to Cliff. He looked at his dad, who was staring blankly at the TV. If he was listening to the conversation, he didn't act like it.

"You need to get him into a place where he can get

constant care," Cliff repeated. Then he walked out of the room. He had only been there for ten minutes.

Jeff nodded his head and shut the front door as Cliff left.

How am I supposed to do that exactly? Who do I call? How can we pay for it? Thanks for nothing, Cliff, he thought.

Jeff hated thinking about money. He didn't want to think about anything. Not about school. Money. Danielle. Help.

He knew all he should be thinking about was his dad.

The phone rang.

OVERLOAD

It was a doctor's office. His dad had an appointment the next day. It was at nine in the morning. Jeff had school. Andrea wouldn't be there until noon. She was staying till five. The last time Jeff's dad came home from Building Up, Andrea was there from twelve to five.

But now? Jeff knew he couldn't leave his dad alone that long.

Jeff asked if they could reschedule the appointment. It was for a PET scan. Jeff Googled it on his iPad as the appointment scheduler was talking. It was a test where doctors looked for diseases in the body. He figured they wanted to know just how far the cancer had spread.

He told the doctor's office they were going to keep the appointment. Jeff figured he would have to miss school.

Again.

He knew he couldn't miss school and keep his grades up. But he didn't have a choice. He told himself it was just this once.

He got off the phone.

It immediately rang again.

It was another doctor's office. They wanted to schedule an MRI. Jeff knew this was where they would examine his dad's brain.

The appointment was for the day after tomorrow. Jeff told them his dad would be there.

He would just have to miss more school.

After that phone call, there was another call a few minutes later. The first doctor's office called. They weren't sure they could do the PET scan. Jeff's dad didn't have the best insurance coverage.

"I thought he had Medicare," Jeff said tensely.

"That only covers so much. Does he have gap coverage?"

Jeff had no idea what that was. He looked at his page of notes from all the phone calls.

He told the lady on the other line that he would speak to his dad and call her back. Then Jeff went to talk to his dad.

He was sleeping.

Jeff went back to the kitchen table and tried to work on calculus. He couldn't concentrate. He wondered if Andrea could change her hours. Maybe she could come in the morning instead.

Jeff knew it would only be a temporary fix.

Andrea's hours would run out soon.

Then it would be Jeff.

Only Jeff.

Taking care of his dad.

He thought about working on something else. Jeff looked in his backpack. He didn't know where to start. His head was spinning.

Jeff Corman was almost seventeen, but he felt like he had aged twenty years in one morning.

Chapter 74

EVEN MORE ALONE

Well, Jeff," Mr. McDonald said. "If you feel that's what you need to do, there will always be a spot for you when your schedule opens up. You can come back any time."

Jeff was quitting the Key Club. He had no idea how this would look on his college résumé. He wanted to know if he could still put it down, but he didn't dare ask.

Jeff paced around the living room as he talked on the phone with his teacher.

He didn't tell Mr. McDonald the reason. He didn't tell him he was stepping back because of his father. Jeff thought the teacher might know what was going on. He thought Brian or Daryl might have told some people. Maybe it had gotten back to Mr. McDonald and the school's administrators.

Shortly after getting off the phone, Jeff got a text from

Brian. "Going to the movies later. If you want to get away for a few hours, we'll come get you. Danielle's coming."

"Get away? Get away?!" Jeff screamed out loud. "There is no getting away! I'll never be free. I'll never have a life of my own. Not until he's dead."

He quickly caught himself.

He knew his dad was sleeping. He hoped he didn't hear him.

Jeff's entire body tensed. He fell onto the couch. He was gritting his teeth. He clenched his fists so tightly he thought he might break his phone.

The tears were coming now. He couldn't stop them. He was trying to be quiet. He was crying so hard he couldn't breathe.

He forced himself to get to his feet.

The door to the house opened.

It was Andrea.

She was dressed in her Building Up uniform.

Without saying a word, she wrapped her arms around him. He hugged her too. He tried not to grip her too hard.

"Relax," Andrea whispered softly. "You're gonna be fine, Jeff. Everything is gonna be okay."

Chapter 75

RESPITE

Andrea organized all the appointments. Somehow she made them fit into her schedule. Then she made Jeff and his dad lunch.

Jeff was still crying. He had so many questions. He had so many fears. He knew he wouldn't be able to do this by himself. His family needed Andrea.

He needed Andrea.

What will happen when her time is up? he thought.

He was sitting at the kitchen table. He'd tried to restart his calculus homework, but his head hurt now. His body felt hot from stress.

"Jeff," Andrea said when she came back into the kitchen. "Can I talk to your dad about going into hospice care?"

"Why?" Jeff asked. He didn't mind Andrea wanting to do that. He just didn't know why she would want to.

"In a lot of these situations, the patient is more will-ing to go when somebody other than a family member tells them they have to."

"Can't he see that he needs to be somewhere else?" Jeff didn't understand why his dad was being so stubborn.

"No, Jeff," Andrea said. "He can't. This is home. Regardless of how he feels physically. This is his home."

Chapter 76

MOMENT

After Andrea left, Jeff studied for an hour.

It was tough. He kept thinking about his future.

Will I finish high school?

Will I have to enroll in adult education and get a GED?

Will I be able to go to a good college and get a good job?

Before he knew it, it was almost nine o'clock.

His dad had stayed in his bedroom.

"You want something to eat?" Jeff asked in one of the few moments his dad was awake. He was watching an old episode of *Cheers*.

"Nah, I'm okay," his dad said.

He stretched out on the couch in his dad's room. He decided he was going to sleep in there that night. In case his dad needed him.

"Jeff," his dad said as Jeff was starting to nod off.

Jeff looked over at him.

"Everything's going to be all right."

"I love you, Dad." Jeff felt himself tearing up.

"I know, Jeff. I love you too."

Jeff stared at his dad. Then he felt himself relax.

Before he knew it, he was asleep.

Chapter 77

HELL, PART 1

Jeff! Jeff!" his dad called.

Jeff was so tired he'd actually fallen into a deep sleep.

As Jeff slowly opened his eyes, he remembered where he was. He remembered what had happened the day before. Then he realized his dad was on the floor, sitting up against the bed. There was a pillow next to him.

"Dad!" Jeff stood up.

"That damn fan," his dad half-laughed. "It was blowing on me. It was hard to breathe. I tried whacking it with a pillow and I fell."

"Why didn't you just yell at me to wake up?"

"You were sleeping."

They stared at each other.

Jeff could see the look of helplessness in his father's eyes. He realized his father wanted him to make some decisions. He realized his father wanted Jeff to be his father, if just for a moment.

"I'm still having trouble breathing."

"You want me to call 9-1-1?" Jeff was going to do it no matter what his dad said.

"Yes."

Jeff took out his phone and called for help. As he did, a wave of relief washed over him.

Chapter 78

THE REAL DEAL

Jeff's dad was taken to the ER. Jeff drove over and saw him lying in a bed. He had oxygen tubes in his nose. But he was awake and alert. More alert than Jeff had seen him in some time.

"He needs twenty-four hour care," Jeff said to the doctor when he came over.

"Yes," the doctor said.

"He never should've been sent home from Building Up." Jeff knew this ER doctor saw a lot of patients and spoke with many people. Jeff didn't care. He was never going to go through what he'd just gone through again. He didn't know how he was going to do it, but he wasn't going to let his dad come home.

"They shouldn't have sent him home." The doctor looked at Jeff's father's chart. "All you need is a signature for that kind of care. Couldn't the other doctors there see that?"

Jeff's dad was admitted to the hospital around two in the morning. Jeff slept between two small chairs across from his father's bed.

Around eight that morning, Dr. Galucci appeared. She worked with Dr. Wilson, who wasn't in yet.

"I spoke with Dr. Wilson, and I looked at all of your father's records," she said solemnly. She stared right at Jeff as she spoke, even though his father was awake. "Given that his cancer is at stage four and looking at his current physical condition, we think it might be time for him to enter a hospice. We don't recommend running more tests."

Hospice.

Jeff knew this wasn't the end. Just another step very close to the end.

With nothing left to say, the doctor left the room. Jeff's father stared at the wall.

He'd gone away again.

Jeff couldn't blame him.

Chapter 79

CIRCLING

Jeff sat with his dad for a while. The two men didn't speak. His father nodded off. Jeff stared at the door to the room.

Eventually, some people from Trinity Hospice Services came to talk to him. There were two women. They talked about what a hospice provided. The goal was to make his father comfortable.

"He can leave you with dignity," the older woman said. She was trying to be as delicate as possible.

Jeff just listened. He wasn't sure he understood everything that was happening. He just knew more people were involved now, whether his dad liked it or not.

As much as Jeff had tried to manage everything, he realized his father needed this. He needed it too. Jeff felt bad making decisions for his dad. He had become the father. His father had become the son.

Nagging questions hit him hard. He couldn't get them out of his mind.

Could I do more?

Should I do more?

Shouldn't I try and save Dad?

Am I being selfish?

Chapter 80

ISLE SHORE

Jeff's dad was going into hospice at a place called Isle Shore.

It was an older facility that looked a lot like Building Up. There was a reception area. Therapy rooms. A cafeteria. And community spaces where patients spent most of their time outside of their own rooms.

Jeff knew this place wasn't as nice as Building Up. But it was clean. And the people were friendly. He also liked it because it was close to their house, close to Cliff, and close to the beach. Jeff's dad had access to twenty-four hour care and pain medication.

Andrea helped Jeff register his dad and set up his room. His dad had come over from the hospital in an ambulance. When Jeff got to his room, Andrea was there talking to him. His dad was on oxygen. There was a tank by the bed.

Jeff knew this situation was permanent. He quickly realized when people got closer to death, they needed help doing the things they used to do on their own. They were no longer self-sufficient.

Danielle had sent Jeff a text to see if he wanted to meet her later. Jeff felt weird saying yes, especially with his dad at Isle Shore. He figured maybe they could come by and visit him. His dad would like that.

"The prodigal son returns." Andrea smiled as Jeff walked into the room.

Jeff smiled back. Andrea was a lovely person. He truly saw her now. She was someone Jeff cared about.

"Hey," Jeff said.

"Hi," Jeff's dad said. He didn't sound too happy.

"Sadly, I need to take my leave of you," Andrea said as she got her purse. "I'll visit you tomorrow. Okay, William?"

Andrea smiled at Jeff and walked out of the room.

"I wanna go home," his dad said as soon as she was gone. "I don't like this place."

"Dad ..." He knew this was coming. "You can't go home. If you do, it will be just like last night. We'll be going right back to the hospital."

"No, it won't." Jeff's dad wasn't yelling. He didn't have the strength for it. He was desperately trying to fight for some trace of his old life. Before he became so helpless.

"I can't take care of you," Jeff said, his voice cracking.

"You can."

"Not like this."

"You can take care of me, Jeff. You did a great job before."

"Before, you weren't so sick, Dad. I'm sorry. I just can't. It's dangerous to have you at home." Jeff wanted to cry, but the tears weren't coming. He was upset, but not as much as he thought he would be.

"We can't afford this place." His dad sat up in bed.

"Andrea worked it out with social services. We may have to eventually sell the house, but it will have to be sold anyway when you ..."

They stared at each other.

This really was the end. It wasn't immediate, but it was closer than it had ever been.

Jeff went over to his dad and hugged him. He started to cry.

"I'm sorry, Dad." He cried even harder. "I'm sorry I can't do more."

"Don't be sorry, son." His dad was crying a little now. "You're a great boy, Jeff. A great son. I love you. This place is all right."

Chapter 81

THE BROTHERS CORMAN

Jeff walked into his dad's room. Uncle Lenny and Uncle Nicholas watched as Cliff fed Jeff's dad a hamburger from In-N-Out Burger. That had always been one of his favorite fast-food restaurants.

"Hi." Jeff smiled.

His uncles hugged him as Cliff finished feeding his father.

"So this is the place," Jeff said.

"Yeah, it's nice." Uncle Nicholas smiled as he looked around the room.

Jeff was waiting for them to say more. To tell him, "Okay, kid, you've done everything you can for our brother. We got it from here."

But that never happened.

Instead, Jeff got peppered with a lot of questions.

Questions he didn't expect. Questions he didn't have any answers to.

"What do you think he needs?"

"What do you want to do?"

"How can we help you?"

It was then Jeff realized how much they appreciated what he'd done for their brother. How much he'd been alone in taking care of him and making decisions.

"I just want him to be okay," Jeff said. He bit his lower lip. He could feel himself getting emotional. He seemed to have more and more of those moments.

"You've done a great job, Jeff," Uncle Lenny said.

"Yeah," Uncle Nicholas agreed. "There aren't too many sixteen-year-old kids who could have done what you did."

Chapter 82

SATURDAY AFTERNOON

Shortly after that conversation, the uncles got a nurse to help their brother get out of bed. Once he was comfortably seated in a wheelchair, they wheeled him outside.

"It's the first time I've been outside in a while," he said breathlessly.

They wheeled him over to a table near a small pond.

Isle Shore may not have been the best place Jeff could have put his dad, but right now it was perfect.

They told stories about when his dad and uncles were younger. How his dad, as the oldest, got in the most trouble. How he used to beat up both his brothers. And how he defended them against neighborhood bullies.

"He did that?" Cliff howled with laughter.

Everybody laughed. Even Jeff's dad.

"I'm tired," he said eventually. "I wanna rest."

"Invite Danielle to lunch," Uncle Nicholas said. "We want to meet this girl. Your dad told us a lot about her already."

"Okay."

Jeff's uncles were going to take him to lunch. Cliff was going home soon. They wheeled Jeff's dad back to his room to rest.

"Wanna eat with my family?" Jeff excitedly texted to Danielle.

"Love to," she wrote back. "Just let me know where. I'll meet you there."

Jeff would text her once he knew where they were going to eat.

Cliff was talking to Jeff's uncles as they walked out the door.

"Jeff?" his dad called in a low voice.

"Yeah, Dad?" Jeff went over to him.

"Is the house okay?"

"Yeah." Jeff almost laughed. He wondered how his dad could care about that when he was so ill. "I'll take some pictures on my phone when I stop off at the house. I'll show you later."

"Yeah, do that." Jeff's dad was looking right at him for the first time in what seemed like forever. "I'd like to see the house. I don't want to wait until I get home again."

"Okay."

Chapter 83

LUNCH

Lunch went really well for Jeff. Danielle sat by his side as they both chatted with his uncles. They talked about colleges. About what they wanted to do with their lives.

"You're the first girlfriend Jeff has introduced us to," Uncle Nicholas joked.

"I was saving the best one," Jeff said.

They all laughed. Danielle was glowing. She knew Jeff thought she was special. He squeezed her soft hand.

After lunch, Jeff and Danielle made plans to hang out later. Then he drove with his uncles back to Isle Shore.

"This is a really nice area," Uncle Lenny said.

Jeff wondered if things would be okay for a while. Maybe his dad would be fine at Isle Shore. Maybe he would have more time.

HELL, PART 2

Ahh …" Jeff's dad was moaning as Jeff and his uncles walked into his room.

They stood around the bed.

Eventually, Jeff's father stopped moaning. His eyes rolled into the back of his head. His lips twitched.

The brothers looked at Jeff.

"He's never done that before." He stared at his dad. He was waiting for him to shake his head. To let whatever happened pass.

"I think he just had a stroke," Uncle Nicholas said.

They called for a nurse.

A male nurse examined him. He checked his eyes with a small flashlight.

"Mr. Corman, can you hear me?" The male nurse stared

into Jeff's father's eyes. Then he stood back and looked at the family. "He's had a stroke."

"What happens now?" Jeff asked.

"Well, the way it works under hospice is that unless the patient asks for it—or his family asks for it—life-saving measures aren't provided. We just make the patient as comfortable as possible until they expire."

The male nurse made some notes on a chart.

"You can let his shift nurses know the course of action you'd like to take." The male nurse nodded at Jeff, then left the room.

Jeff felt himself starting to get upset again. "Just when I got him somewhere safe," he said.

Uncle Lenny put his hand on Jeff's shoulder. Jeff wanted to cry but didn't think it would do any good.

Chapter 85

WAITING

For the next two days, Jeff sat with his uncles at his father's bedside. His dad continued to sleep as the nurses came in intermittently and gave him pain medication.

The brothers told Jeff more stories about his dad. Jeff learned his dad had stolen a car once. He took his younger brothers out for a ride and then returned the car before anybody knew it was gone. Jeff couldn't believe it.

He loved hearing their stories. The only problem was they didn't last forever. Jeff knew eventually there would be no more stories to tell about his dad. And then what?

Cliff still visited Isle Shore too. Whenever he did, he talked to Jeff's dad like he was conscious. Like nothing was wrong. As futile as that seemed, Jeff appreciated it. Cliff was a great friend.

Chapter 86

THE BIG QUESTION

The uncles had gone out to get everyone something to eat.

Jeff stared at his dad. His mouth was hanging open. It had been since his stroke. He seemed to be in the deepest sleep.

Another nurse came in. She was young. She had short blonde hair and tattoos.

Jeff had a thought. "Can we give him water?" he asked.

He wanted his dad to live. He wanted to give him every chance. He didn't want him to suffer. That was his biggest fear. That somehow, even with all the layers of medication they were giving him, his dad was in pain.

"You can do that," the nurse said. "But it will only prolong his agony."

"Agony?" Jeff asked. "I thought he wasn't in any pain."

"He's not. But if he is in any pain and can't wake up, a life-saving measure will only extend the pain until he expires. Unless, of course, he can come out of it on his own."

Jeff looked at his dad.

He wanted to tell the nurse he didn't just want to let him die. That he wanted to fight for him. Then he thought about something Andrea had said. About how having surgery was her key to freedom from the body she had been assigned at birth.

As much as Jeff loved his dad, was there any chance he could save him? Or was this horrible situation Jeff's key to freedom?

Jeff hated having to make these tough choices. There was no way to prepare for them. No way to make the right decision. No way to know which was the right one.

The nurse had long since left the room.

Jeff still didn't know what to do.

Chapter 87

GOODBYE

On the third day after the stroke, Jeff bumped into Andrea as she was leaving Jeff's father's room. It was early evening, and the last rays of sunlight were streaming in. As he slept, his dad made gasping noises.

"I tried to get over here sooner," Andrea said. "They switched my hours at Building Up."

"Should I be doing more?" Jeff asked.

"Jeff." Andrea put her hand on his shoulder and looked at his father. "You've done so much for your father. Despite everything, he's very ill."

Jeff nodded his head. He wiped some tears from his eyes.

"You have nothing to question yourself about. No matter how you may feel inside. Your father is proud of you. He knows you love him. He's excited for your future."

Jeff liked that Andrea talked about him in the present

tense. Earlier that day, one of the hospice workers had said that today would probably be the day Jeff's dad died. Unless there was a drastic change.

"But he's not gonna see any of my future," Jeff whispered.

"He will." Andrea squeezed his shoulder.

They stood there for a long time, not saying anything. Eventually, Andrea hugged Jeff and left him alone with his dad.

Jeff stood there. Alone. He stared at his dad. He wanted to shake him. He wanted to beg him to fight harder for his life. He wanted his dad to come back to him. But he was almost gone for good now.

"I love you so much, Dad," Jeff cried. "I'm gonna miss you so much."

His dad made a loud noise. It wasn't like the gasping one from the day of the stroke. It sounded like he said go.

"Dad?" Jeff leaned closer. "Do you want me to leave?"

His father made another noise. It might not have sounded like much to anybody else, but it sure sounded like something to Jeff.

"Yes."

Jeff took a deep breath. He kissed his father on the forehead and gave him a hug. Jeff didn't want to let go.

So he didn't.

Until he was ready.

Chapter 88

THE CALL

It was 3:16 a.m. when the call came.

Jeff was in a deep sleep. Danielle had come over earlier. They watched a movie and cuddled on the couch. They both knew they didn't need to do much more than that.

Jeff was in his bedroom. He stared at his phone before he picked it up. He wasn't sure he was ready to hear what he knew he would hear.

"Hello?" Jeff cleared his throat.

"Mr. Corman?" a nurse asked.

"Yes."

"Your father, he—"

"I know," Jeff said.

He spoke with the nurse for a little while longer.

Jeff's dad had prepaid his own funeral. All Jeff had to

do was call the mortuary, and they would take care of his father's body.

After talking with the nurse, Jeff wept. As bad as he felt, he was thankful his dad had told Andrea how proud he was of Jeff. He was so grateful his dad knew how much Jeff loved him.

Chapter 89

ARRANGEMENTS

According to Jewish law, when a person dies, they should be buried as soon as possible. Jeff's dad was going to be buried less than two days after his death.

The Cormans weren't very religious. They didn't go to the synagogue much. In fact, after Jeff had his bar mitzvah at thirteen, they didn't really go at all.

Still, Jeff was Jewish, so he spent the next morning after his father's death talking with Rabbi Berkowitz from their synagogue. He was going to perform the service.

"I know you are in pain," the rabbi told him. "However, when somebody dies, they are no longer bound by space and time. So in many ways, your father will be with us in a much stronger way. His *neshama*, his soul, will be with us."

Jeff didn't remember too much from his limited time at Hebrew school.

He liked that idea, though. He also felt good when the rabbi told him how his dad and mom were now reunited for eternity. Someday—hopefully many years from now—Jeff wanted to join them.

Jeff and his uncles were standing at the checkout line at the grocery store. They were buying some things for the "meal of condolence" after the funeral. They had plates, cups, napkins, soft drinks, and coffee.

As they waited in line, Jeff looked at his uncles. They looked tired. And listless. Losing their brother was hitting them both hard at the same time.

Jeff had been so close to everything. Seeing what his father was going through every day for years had prepared him.

"How are you guys?" he asked.

His uncles looked at him.

"Well, I'm sad." Lenny shrugged. He tried to force a smile.

"Yeah ..." Uncle Nicholas's listless look remained.

"I'm sorry," Jeff said. "I know my dad loved you guys."

Uncle Lenny and Uncle Nicholas both stared at Jeff. Their vacant expressions vanished. They seemed to only see Jeff as his own man now. At that moment Jeff loved and felt closer to his uncles than he ever had before.

ALONE WITH DANIELLE

Jeff thought writing his dad's eulogy was going to be hard.

It wasn't.

He'd always liked writing. He looked at the eulogy like a writing assignment. The most important assignment he would probably ever write.

Jeff started by writing everything down about his dad that he could remember. Then he narrowed it down to some key points.

He turned that into a few paragraphs. Accepting that it wouldn't be perfect. Accepting that he wasn't really saying goodbye. Jeff told himself he was done.

Then he went over to Danielle's house.

Danielle and Jeff walked in the cool night air. The holidays were around the corner. And then New Year's.

The first time Jeff had ever celebrated the season without either parent.

He was an orphan. He told himself not to think about it.

Instead, he focused on Danielle. How beautiful she was. How good she was for him. How snugly she had her arm wrapped around his. How they could walk together and not say anything and that was okay.

Jeff turned and gave her a spontaneous hug. He felt her heart beating against his chest. He felt connected to her.

"Thank you," he whispered in her ear. "Thank you for not giving up on me."

They both continued to whisper special things to each other.

Eventually, this night would be over. The funeral would be tomorrow. Then there would be paperwork to submit. He would need help with his father's estate. Figure out the finances.

Again, Jeff told himself not to think about it. This moment with Danielle was what mattered.

Chapter 91

FUNERAL

The service was held outside. There was a makeshift canopy set up for the small gathering of mourners to sit under. Across from that was a small podium with a microphone. Near that was a simple wood coffin on a pedestal. There was an open grave with a dirt mound next to it.

"It is very easy in times like this to look at our lives and wonder why," Rabbi Berkowitz said. "However, Hashem has a plan. And while our faith in that plan is tested in these moments, it is also our faith that ultimately allows us to pass this test."

Jeff was sitting between his uncles. Cliff was next to Lenny. Jeff made sure Danielle, Brian, and Daryl were sitting behind him, along with their families. Many of Jeff's teachers were also in attendance.

"And now William's son, Jeff, is going to say a few words."

Jeff took a deep breath, clutched the eulogy he'd hand-written, and walked to the podium. As he made his way there, he saw many old family friends with their children, like the Goldbergs. These were families he'd spent weekends with when he was a kid. They were the same people who had drifted away after his mother died.

You can be here for my dad's death, he thought. *But what about his life after my mom died. Where were you when we needed you the most?*

As quickly as those thoughts entered Jeff's head, they were gone. He knew he didn't need to think that way. He knew being mad at people wasn't going to get him anywhere. He refused to be bitter.

Now. Jeff Corman had to live for now.

"My dad was bigger than life when I was a little boy," he said into the microphone. "In the way fathers are to their sons. It wasn't until my mom passed away that we were forced to become closer than father and son. He wasn't well for many of the last years of his life. And while I felt burdened at times by having to always be there for him, I have come to realize what I was asked to do wasn't a burden at all. It was an honor."

Jeff's voice cracked after he said that. He felt like he was about to lose it. About to break down in front of everyone. But somehow he kept his composure and talked about his late father. He told stories about when he was a kid. And about things that had only recently happened.

Then he was done. He looked out at his uncles, his father's friends, his friends, his teachers, and the families he had grown up with. Everyone stood. And then they applauded.

Chapter 92

CLOSURE

I'm so sorry I wasn't more involved," a family friend said to Jeff after the funeral. "I always meant to call your dad. I always meant to check up on you guys."

"It's okay," Jeff said.

He was greeted by people who wanted to tell him stories about his dad. People who had known his mother and father for years before Jeff was born.

Eventually, Jeff found Danielle. He took her hand. They started walking with everyone out of the cemetery. It was time to go back to Jeff's house for the meal of condolence.

"I wish we could just go somewhere and be alone," he said. "Go to the beach or something."

"There'll be plenty of time for that later." She smiled. "You know we need to do this."

We.

Jeff really felt like he and Danielle were a team. He wanted that feeling to last forever.

Andrea walked up to them. She was wearing a simple black dress. She looked like she'd had her hair done.

Jeff was happy to see her. "You look really nice," he said.

"Thank you." Andrea smiled as she gave him a hug.

It wasn't weird for Jeff to hug her. She offered comfort.

"Your eulogy was perfect," Andrea said. "Danielle, who knew Jeff could write and speak so eloquently? His speech brought many to tears."

"You did great, babe," Danielle agreed.

"Thank you." Jeff smiled.

He wanted to say more. He had to say more.

"Thank you for everything you did, Andrea. Thank you for what you did for my father. You made his life so much better with everything you did. He taught me a lot, and you taught me a lot too."

Jeff and Andrea stared at each other. Once she was his enemy. He didn't understand her at all. But ultimately, they were partners in caring for his dad.

"It was my pleasure." Andrea put her hand on her chest. "I hope you don't think this is goodbye."

"I don't want it to be."

"It isn't. Why don't we all head back to the house now?" Andrea smiled.

"Okay."

All three of them walked together. They didn't say anything. They just let the somberness of the moment speak for them.

With every passing step, Jeff realized he was on his own.

No mother.

No father.

Just Jeff Corman, standing on his own two feet and facing whatever life had to offer.

But he took comfort in the fact that he wasn't alone. Not really. He had his uncles. He had Cliff. He had Andrea. And most importantly, he had Danielle. He also knew he could handle whatever life threw at him.

He looked up at the sky and mouthed *Thank You* to the infinite heavens.

WANT TO KEEP READING?

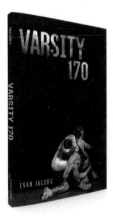

Turn the page for a sneak peek at another book from the Gravel Road series: Evan Jacobs's *Varsity 170*.

ISBN: 978-1-62250-889-1

CHAPTER 1

BEST FRIENDS

You have Miss Scalf for English. Right?" Marcus's voice crackled a bit over Chad's earbud.

"Yeah, you do too. Right?" Chad turned the steering wheel into Marcus's tract.

The best friends were going to see each other in a few minutes. But they both saw no reason why they shouldn't be talking on the phone now. One of their favorite '80s songs, Journey's "Only the Young," was playing in the car through Chad's iPod. They often worked out to this song. They first heard it in the movie *Vision Quest*. It was a wrestling movie, one of their favorites.

"Dude, I'm almost there. Don't make me wait," Chad said. He disconnected the call and cranked the music.

Chad Erickson and Marcus Pagel had been best friends

since kindergarten. Today was the first day of their senior year. They had worked their entire lives for this moment. It was going to be the best year yet.

It had to be.

In nine months they were going to graduate. Marcus was headed to a four-year college. He didn't know where he was going yet: Stanford, UCLA, Washington. But wherever he went, he was going to wrestle. Chad wanted to go to a four-year school too. He had applied to Stanford and a few others. But he didn't think he would get in.

"I'm going to college," he would tell his girlfriend, Maria. "But I might have to go to a community college first."

There was still an outside chance that a scout from one of the Pac-12 colleges would see him. He'd be impressed with Chad. Scoop him up. Give him a full scholarship. Then Chad would wrestle for that school. And win.

That was Chad's dream since his sophomore year. But so far, it hadn't happened. Chad's parents didn't have a lot of money. Neither did Marcus's. Chad knew going to a four-year school right out of high school would be too expensive. Marcus didn't seem to care about the money.

He pulled up outside of Marcus's two-story home.

Chad had practically grown up here. He was another son. Just one of the family. He could help himself to their food, or get himself a drink. Nobody would blink. Not even Marcus's little brother, Dave.

Chad sat there for a second. He thought about turning off his car and going inside.

But he didn't. Instead, he pressed a couple of buttons on his iPod and replayed "Only the Young" from the beginning. This way Marcus could listen to it too.

They weren't late. Yet. But if he went inside, Marcus would no doubt try to show him some YouTube video that Marcus and Dave found hilarious. Chad was an only child. He envied the relationship that Marcus had with his brother. Dave was a cool kid for an eighth grader. And he idolized Chad and Marcus.

"I'm gonna wrestle when I get to high school," Dave would say. "Just like you guys."

Suddenly, the red door to the Pagel house flew open. Marcus bounded outside. He had his backpack slung over his shoulder, a huge smile on his face. He was wearing dark jeans and a Shepard High School sweatshirt.

"Sup, sup!" he yelled across the driveway.

Chad smiled and waved to him. Marcus's mom and Dave appeared in the doorway. Chad could tell by Dave's smile that Marcus was probably teasing his mom before he walked out of the house.

"Marcus," she called in a hushed voice. "You're gonna wake up half the block!"

"Sorry, Mom!" Marcus hollered back. His mom's face dropped as he walked backward, looking at her. "I'm just saying hi to my boy. You and Dad always taught me to be a polite little boy!"

Dave started laughing even more, and this made Chad laugh too.

Then Marcus dropped to the ground.

Here, Evan is recording a voice for his animated horror film, Insect.

ABOUT THE AUTHOR

Evan Jacobs was born in Long Island, New York. His family moved to California when he was four years old. They settled in Fountain Valley, where he still lives today.

As a filmmaker, Evan has directed eleven low-budget films. He has also had various screenplays produced and realized by other directors. He co-wrote the film *Knockout*, starring "Stone Cold" Steve Austin. He is currently juggling several movie and book projects. Evan recently started Anhedenia Films TV. This YouTube channel (YouTube. com/anhedeniafilmz) showcases his work in animation.

Evan is also a behavior interventionist for people who have special needs. He works with a variety of students to make their days as successful as possible. His third young adult novel, *Screaming Quietly,* won a Moonbeam Children's Book Award bronze medal. You can find out more about him at www.anhedeniafilms.blogspot.com.